Firelight winked on the dark, empty desert in front of him.

Raider dropped belly down onto a sharp rock, the breath driven out of him.

The rifle slug hit the ground twenty yards in front of him.

Raider's Remington was in his hand.

But he had no damn target.

He rolled off the rock that was poking into his gut, but he didn't stand.

The gunman was out in front of him.

Somewhere.

Blocking Raider's way to the Colorado River and safety.

Who, damn it?

And why?

Other books in the *RAIDER* series by
J. D. HARDIN

RAIDER
SIXGUN CIRCUS
THE YUMA ROUNDUP
THE GUNS OF EL DORADO
THIRST FOR VENGEANCE
DEATH'S DEAL
VENGEANCE RIDE
CHEYENNE FRAUD
THE GULF PIRATES
TIMBER WAR
SILVER CITY AMBUSH
THE NORTHWEST RAILROAD WAR
THE MADMAN'S BLADE
WOLF CREEK FEUD
BAJA DIABLO
STAGECOACH RANSOM
RIVERBOAT GOLD
WILDERNESS MANHUNT
SINS OF THE GUNSLINGER
BLACK HILLS TRACKDOWN
GUNFIGHTER'S SHOWDOWN
THE ANDERSON VALLEY SHOOT-OUT
BADLANDS PATROL
THE YELLOWSTONE THIEVES
THE ARKANSAS HELLRIDER
BORDER WAR
THE EAST TEXAS DECEPTION
DEADLY AVENGERS
HIGHWAY OF DEATH
THE PINKERTON KILLERS
TOMBSTONE TERRITORY
MEXICAN SHOWDOWN
THE CALIFORNIA KID
BORDER LAW
HANGMAN'S LAW
FAST DEATH

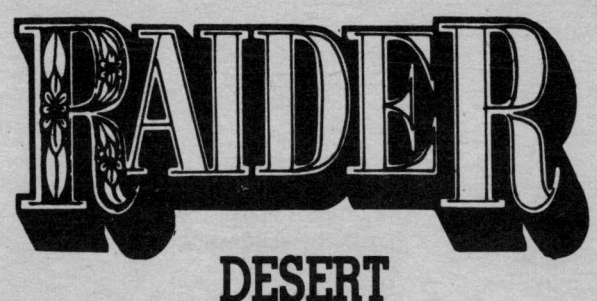

DESERT DEATH TRAP

B
BERKLEY BOOKS, NEW YORK

DESERT DEATH TRAP

A Berkley Book/published by arrangement with
the author

PRINTING HISTORY
Berkley edition/July 1990

All rights reserved.
Copyright © 1990 by The Berkley Publishing Group.
This book may not be reproduced in whole or in part,
by mimeograph or any other means, without permission.
For information address: The Berkley Publishing Group,
200 Madison Avenue, New York, New York 10016.

ISBN: 0-425-12175-5

A BERKLEY BOOK® TM 757,375
Berkley Books are published by The Berkley Publishing Group,
200 Madison Aveunue, New York, New York 10016.
The name "BERKLEY" and the "B" logo
are trademarks belonging to the Berkley Publishing Corporation.

PRINTED IN THE UNITED STATES OF AMERICA

10 9 8 7 6 5 4 3 2 1

DESERT DEATH TRAP

CHAPTER ONE

Raider smiled and kept his eyes closed. Talk about a stroke of luck! Except it wasn't only his luck that was being stroked.

He lay on his belly, the lumpy hotel mattress hard against his erection, and concentrated on the sensations that threatened to overwhelm his nerve endings.

Ah, that was a wisp of cool, soft hair. And another there. And that was a tongue tip. And another down there.

He smiled again, then turned over and opened his eyes so he could watch what was going on and enjoy that, too.

The girl's pretty face turned toward him with a smile.

Then the other one did too.

Ah, sisters. Bless 'em.

They weren't twins, he didn't think, but they looked enough alike that they might have been.

He wasn't sure about it because neither Nina nor Nita

had enough English to tell him, and he damn sure didn't have enough Spanish to figure it out.

Not that they needed to be able to talk to him. They were doing just fine the way things were.

Mm, mmm.

Nina was the one on his left. He thought. Or maybe that one was Nita. Didn't really matter. Her head dipped low while her hands pulled his legs apart and she began to lick his balls, while Nita, or maybe it was Nina, ran her tongue up and down his shaft.

Both of them had long, dark, gleamingly healthy hair that they wore loose so it covered him and tickled and added just that much extra to what they were so busy doing.

Helluva pair, Nina and Nita. They were both built to be wasteful. If, that is, a man believed in the old saying that more than a mouthful was wasted.

They had tits like soft ripe melons and broad, rounded butts. A little thick in the thighs and short-waisted. But a guy could forgive them a few faults.

Mostly what they had was eagerness.

Raider smiled again, but the sisters didn't see. They were too intent on what they were doing to be looking at him now.

Fan-damn-tastic.

He reached down and fondled the back of Nita's neck, then stroked Nina's cheek.

Wow!

Both of them moved upward a few inches so that now Nina was nibbling on the underside of his dick while Nita slurped the head of it noisily into her warm, mobile mouth.

Helluva pair, all right. They'd been having supper at the table next to his in the cafe and did some conspicuous whispering before they began flirting with him.

The lack of a language in common hadn't hampered things a bit.

And Raider had lost his appetite for lingering over pie and coffee on the spot.

A few winks and grins and it had seemed just about the most natural thing in the world that the girls would get up from their table at the same time that he left his.

They slid over, one on each side, and practically started groping him right there in public.

Raider had done the decent thing and paid for their meals too when he paid for his own.

But that had been the only money involved.

Damn, these Arizona-style Mexican girls were something.

This was just about as good as things got.

Nita turned and gave him a pout when he pulled her off him and drew her up on the bed at his side. Nina followed, and pretty soon he had one girl snug against each side of him and both his hands filled with soft, satiny breasts.

The girls giggled and licked his chest, working on each side of him and rimming his nipples with their tongues while their fingers twined and got in each other's way as they both tried to fondle and tease him at the same time.

Raider grinned and maybe groaned a little.

Nina said something to the other one, and both of them lifted up.

They moved down, Nita straddling him on her knees and poising over him while Nina's hand guided him into her sister.

Nita lowered herself until Raider was socketed nice and deep and warm inside her, then Nina burrowed behind and below Nita and began licking Raider's balls again while Nita pumped up and down on him.

Raider took a handful of Nita's breast and squeezed. The girl smiled, her brown eyes alight with pleasure. He reached over and found Nina's vee with his free hand. She was sopping wet there, her juices caught in the thick, black thatch of pubic hair. He slipped two fingers inside her and had room left over for more. He found the button of her pleasure and began to knead it with his thumb.

Nina shuddered and came, her pussy getting even wetter than it had been.

Nita smiled and looked down and said something. After a moment she lifted up off Raider and the two girls switched places, Nina pumping away on top of him now while Nita sucked his balls gently and Raider played with her clit the same way he just had Nina's.

He felt the rising surge of insistent pleasure and tried to hold it back, wanting to hang on to this as long as he could, but the girls were just too damn good for that.

He groaned and felt the long, pumping flow begin.

Nina pressed down hard on top of him, bracing herself on his chest, and he could feel a series of sharp, deliberate contractions around the base of his cock as Nina did something almighty interesting with her muscles there. She had the kind of control that a twenty-dollar whore would have to envy. And at the same time Nina was doing that, Nita was sucking and pulling on his balls so that he felt surrounded by the sensations they were giving him, like he was floating in a tub of sheer pleasure.

He came twice as long and three times as hard as anybody has a right to.

And wished it'd been for even longer.

"Whee-ow!" He grinned up at Nina.

After a moment Nita allowed his right ball to slide out of her mouth, leaving the poor shriveled thing cooling in the air. She laughed and said something to her sister, and Nina laughed too.

Raider hoped they were ready for more of the same. Another minute or so and he damn sure would be.

Seconds, thirds ... hell a guy could spend a whole night doing this and never quit wanting more.

He stroked Nina's side and she giggled. It must have tickled. Nita hadn't come yet, but there was plenty of time enough to take care of that little detail.

He could . . .

A footstep sounded on the hardwood floor just outside his door, the very faint sound of it lost almost at once as the girls began talking to each other.

Nina was still on top of him. He was still lodged very much inside her, his own juices and hers mingling and flowing together down onto him now where the moisture felt almost cold as the drying air reached it. Nita was tickling the sensitive patch of skin between his balls and his ass and saying something to Nina in a voice that was slightly louder than necessary.

Raider bit back the laughter that was trying to erupt from him but wasn't able to keep his belly from convulsing with it.

That was all right. Neither girl seemed to notice.

Shit, he knew what was coming next.

The girls were paying attention to each other, jabbering away in Spanish, and now both of them were playing with his balls.

Raider chuckled softly and reached for the big .44 Remington that was hanging handy on the bedpost just as the hotel room door burst open with a crash.

Raider had carefully locked that door himself not forty-five minutes ago. Nina or Nita had just as carefully unlocked it when he wasn't looking.

A middle-aged Anglo with gray in his mustache and a pipsqueak nickel-plated rimfire revolver in his right hand stood there with fury written all over his face.

The man was all set to play the game, all right. He came storming in, claiming his . . . what? Wives? Sure, why not both of them as his wives? This was, after all, northern Arizona, where there were plenty of Mormons around who might want to claim both girls as wives. So all right, it was his multiple wives that Raider was fooling with.

The guy's pride was no doubt wounded. Grievously

wounded. And wouldn't Raider's wife and employer be interested to hear how he acted when he was away from home on business.

Except Raider didn't have a wife to worry about, and he didn't much give a shit if somebody told Allan Pinkerton that his best operative liked to fuck. Allan was a straitlaced Scotsman, but that didn't necessarily mean that everybody else in the wide world had to be too.

This was an old con and a tired one, but it was apparently still an effective one if the right sucker was told that the offended husband could be dissuaded from reporting the poor sap's indiscretions. For a consideration. In cash.

Raider laughed.

The man standing in the doorway didn't.

But then, the man in the doorway was peering into the muzzle of a well-worn Remington revolver that was being aimed by a large, lean man with a shock of black hair and a sweeping black mustache.

Nina and Nita seemed not to realize yet that things had turned sour. They were going into their act now, screeching and blubbering and trying to cover themselves.

"We didn't mean it, honey."

"Honest, Harry, he practically made us come up here with him."

"You know it's you that we love, honey."

"Please don't beat us, Harry."

Golly gee. Ol' Nina and Nita suddenly knew how to talk English.

Except ol' Harry's bluster had disappeared right along with the color in his face, and he was paying much more attention to the Remington than to the lines he was supposed to be saying.

Raider chuckled and winked at the man.

Nina had tumbled off him, leaving him limp and wet and sticky, when she went into her part of the act. Both girls were huddled at the side of the bed, hugging each other and leaking crocodile tears and pretending to be scared.

Raider sat upright on his side of the bed, the gaping muzzle of the .44 never wavering off its mark in the vicinity of Harry's belly button.

"Come inside, Harry. Shut the door behind you."

The girls finally realized that things weren't as they expected. They shut up and looked first at Harry, then at Raider. One of them—Nina? he thought so—frowned, and both of them sighed and wiped the phony tears off their faces. They were both still pretty, Raider thought. Talented, too.

Harry's mouth worked emptily for a moment. He didn't know quite what to say now. This wasn't what he'd expected. He finally closed his jaw and stepped into the room, pushing the door shut behind him.

"You gonna use that thing in your hand, Harry? Or did you just take it out to polish?"

Harry looked down, realized he was still holding the pipsqueak gun, and acted like he didn't know how to get out of the situation now that he'd gone and created it.

Raider grinned again. "It's okay for you to move enough to put that thing away," he said.

Harry looked grateful. Moving with slow and elaborate care he transferred the rimfire into his coat pocket and let go of it.

"Now let me see," Raider said thoughtfully. "You married to these lovely girls, are you?"

"Uh, yes."

"Then you're a lucky man, Harry," Raider said agreeably.

"Yes, uh, thank you."

Raider smiled. The Remington was still pointed toward Harry's middle.

"I got to give you credit, Harry. You and your ladies are right honorable, so to speak. Most generally with this sort of deal the door busts open before anything much happens. Least you and your ladies drain a man a couple times before you extract your pay."

Harry gave the girls a look that was a mixture of anger tinged with nervousness. After all, Raider still was holding that gun. But as Raider expected, the man didn't like hearing that his whores had given full value. And if Raider had exaggerated just how much fun he'd had time for with the sisters, well, he didn't see any reason why he should be all that concerned about what Harry liked or didn't like.

"You want to know where you can reach my boss, Harry?"

"Uh, no. I . . . don't think that would be . . . necessary. Thank you."

"Whatever pleases you, Harry." Raider grinned at him.

"I think . . . I think I would like to, uh, take my wives and . . . leave now?" Ol' Harry sure did seem intent on looking down the front end of the Remington. The man acted like he'd hardly ever seen such a thing before.

"You come here to get paid off first, didn't you, Harry?" Raider suggested.

The greasy confidence man hesitated, acting like he was going to deny it. Then, with a look of thorough misery, he decided—wisely—that it might be better to be caught in no lies at the moment. He nodded. And swallowed. Hard.

Raider grinned again. "Fair is fair, Harry, and I don't begrudge nobody an honest living." He stood, the muzzle of the revolver remaining trained on Harry's middle, as if the dark steel weapon had a mind of its own, and crossed the few steps to the chair where he had dropped his jeans just a little while earlier. "You can go ahead and get dressed now, girls," he said over his shoulder. He heard a flurry of movement as Nina and Nita began scrambling to get into their dresses.

Raider dipped into a pocket for his loose change and extracted two coins, glanced down to make sure they were what he wanted, and ambled over to stand in front of Harry, the muzzle of the .44 almost pressing against the con man's stomach at that distance.

"Ready to go home to hubby now, ladies?"

"Yes," one of them hissed. Funny how she didn't sound so hot and horny and eager all of a sudden.

"Thanks for the good time, girls," he said politely.

He pressed a pair of silver two-bit pieces into Harry's reluctant hand, then stood back to give them all room to get the hell out of his hotel room.

"G'night, all."

Harry turned, his face pale and sweat-streaked, and snatched the door open.

The three of them fled into the hallway like the hounds of hell were snapping at their heels.

And come to that, maybe they were.

Raider closed the door behind them and carefully pushed the bolt home.

"You dumb cunts. What made you pick him for a mark?" he heard thinly from the hallway. "You think we're in this for fun or something? You think you're supposed to pick marks that you *want* to fuck? Jeez." Harry sounded disgusted. His voice was receding rapidly toward the lobby.

Raider chuckled as he bent to collect his clothes. After so enjoyable an evening, a nightcap was definitely in order, he thought.

CHAPTER TWO

It wasn't particularly late. The encounter with Nina and Nita and their now unhappy cohort had begun at supper and hadn't lasted nearly as long as Raider had intended. A glance at the wall clock in the hotel lobby showed him it was barely past eight. He smiled to himself. The time hadn't been all that long, but it had been mighty well spent. He felt drained now and completely relaxed.

He crossed the lobby—a tall, lean man dressed in his customary jeans and boots and scuffed leather jacket, with a flat-crowned black Stetson tugged low over dark, piercing eyes and a loose, catlike grace in his movements—and stopped at the desk clerk's counter.

There was no sign of the man on duty, so Raider tapped lightly on the bell provided beside the registration book. He could hear the scrape of a chair on the floor inside a small private office behind the counter, and a moment later the clerk showed up with half a biscuit in his hand.

"Sorry to interrupt your dinner, friend," Raider apologized. "Has my party checked in yet?"

"No, sir, Mr. Raider, not yet. But I'll let you know as soon as he comes in."

Raider shrugged and gave the friendly clerk a rueful smile. "Thanks."

"No bother. I'll let you know right away. I promise. It, uh, won't likely be tonight, though. The last coach has already unloaded its passengers. There won't be another until early tomorrow morning."

"Damn," Raider muttered. "Thanks anyway." He turned and drifted toward the saloon that was attached to the lobby in lieu of a hotel restaurant. More profit in liquor for the traveling businessmen who passed through Chloride than in food, Raider guessed.

Chloride, Arizona, was a town that seemed to cater to the needs of those who were passing through—if only because there would be little enough reason for anyone to settle down and stay. It was on the stage route between Flagstaff to the east and the Tonopah and Goldfield discoveries in Nevada to the west.

From one of those to the next, though, there wasn't a helluva lot to see except wheel tracks and Chloride.

Why the client wanted to meet Raider here . . . Well, it was his own affair, of course. As the guy who was footing the bill he was entitled.

The telegraph message from Chicago had been specific. The Pinkerton National Detective Agency's top operative was to proceed to Chloride, Arizona, and check into the Crown Hotel. He would be met there by the client, whose name was Arnold Phipps. The telegram hadn't said exactly what the case would be.

And no damned wonder that bit of information was omitted, too.

It hadn't occurred to Raider until he was already in Chloride sitting on his thumbs and waiting for Phipps to show up—he frankly wouldn't likely have accepted the job if he'd remembered it beforehand—but he had heard about this Phipps before in the form of office gossip.

It was a dreary little missing-persons case that Phipps kept coming back to and reopening every time he got enough money together to pay the Pinkerton fees.

The story was as dreary as Phipps's hopes could be by this time. Years back, Phipps's daughter had got herself knocked up by a passing dandy. Papa Phipps gave the girl a thrashing and told her to get the hell out, which she up and did, taking off presumably in search of the short-time boyfriend. She hadn't been heard from since.

Now the dumb SOB, having successfully sent the girl away, had gone and developed second thoughts about running off his daughter and only grandbaby.

Now he wanted the two of them—or three in the event the girl had found the boyfriend and browbeat him into making an honest woman of her—found and brought happily home to Grampa's bosom.

Raider's opinion was that the girl and kid were probably better off the way they were.

Not that Arnold Phipps or Allan Pinkerton either one was consulting him on the subject. What Phipps wanted was for the girl and child—he or she or it would be four or thereabouts by now—found. What Allan wanted was for Phipps to pay his bill on time, which the guy obviously did or Pinkerton wouldn't keep coming back to the ho-hum case.

What Raider wanted was to get out of this useless assignment. Missing persons just wasn't his kind of case. It was dull work, and he plain didn't like it.

Things must be almighty slow in Chicago right now, he suspected, or Allan wouldn't have pointed the finger at him about it. The damned Scotsman just couldn't abide for one of his operatives to sit around enjoying himself and drawing pay, though. Not if there was a penny to be squeezed out of people like this Phipps.

So Raider had been sent to Chloride—and why here, damn it?—to wait for Phipps to show up and make another attempt to find the darling daughter.

To cap the whole, wonderful thing off, the girl was supposed to be of the same approximate degree of beauty as a young sow in a mud wallow. Or so the office rumors went among those who claimed to have seen a photograph that Phipps always carried.

Raider was less than thrilled by the prospects of this one.

Oh, well, he thought. At least he'd had Nina and Nita for a temporary diversion while he was waiting. That had to be worth something for a fella's frame of mind.

He yawned his way into the saloon, ordered a beer, and carried it to an empty table. There were a couple of card games in progress nearby, low-stakes affairs played by travelers who were stopping in town for the night and wanted to pass the time while they waited for the next leg of their journey. Raider thought he might have a beer or two and then maybe sit in on a game. There sure wasn't anything better to do.

"Pssst!"

Raider glanced up from his cards. He really didn't mind the interruption. This hand was going nowhere, which seemed to be the way his luck was consistently running tonight. Not that his losses were threatening to break him, though. At sixty cents down he was the big loser at the table. The play was what you might call casual.

"Me?" he mouthed silently.

The man at the door nodded and motioned for Raider to come.

Raider shrugged and held up a finger to tell the fellow to wait a moment. He took one last look at the hopeless muddle of mixed trash he'd been dealt and tossed the cards face-down onto the table. "I'm out, gentlemen."

No one seemed to mind. "If you have something better to do, friend," one of them said, "then I envy you." That brought a round of smiles from the other players, who were just as bored, and Raider scooped his loose change into a pocket.

He stood and ambled over to the doorway. The man who had beckoned to him was still standing there in plain sight with both hands in view.

Raider was sure he'd never seen the man before. The fellow seemed inoffensive enough—pudgy and on the short side, with a struggling wisp of mustache and a cloth cap perched on top of limp, greasy hair. If the man was armed with anything more deadly than a toothpick it didn't show.

"Mmm?"

"You're Raider?" His voice was held to a whisper, and his eyes kept darting past Raider's shoulder as if he was anxious that they not be overheard.

"That's right."

"I need to talk to you."

"Correct me if I'm wrong, but I think you're doing that already."

"In private," the plump man insisted.

Far as Raider could see there wasn't anybody in Chloride who would give a shit if the two of them stood in the street and shouted. But why not? "Yeah, okay."

He followed the fellow out into the street and around a corner into a dark alley.

Raider's expression turned a trifle grim. If the guy was thinking he could be set up this easy . . .

There was no need for alarm, and the Remington in Raider's holster wasn't touched. The alley was empty except for some sunbaked litter and the two men.

"You're with the Pinkertons, ain't you?"

Raider nodded. There wasn't any reason that he knew of to keep it a secret around here. "That's right."

"Are the Pinkertons still offering a reward for Jonas Dial?" the short man whispered.

Raider's interest quickened. Right damn now.

Jonas Dial was the most wanted son of a bitch on the

list at the moment. And not just the Pinkerton list either. *Every*body wanted a piece of the elusive Mr. Dial—the Pinkerton Agency, Wells Fargo, the U.S. Department of Justice, roughly half the railroads doing business west of the Mississippi . . . shit, everybody.

Dial was the most successful robber to come down the pike in years. The sort that songs and legends would grow around if he wasn't brought down soon.

He worked with only a handful of trusted and damned well trained men. Often enough he worked completely alone. He struck quick, hard, and too, too well. And promptly disappeared again.

No one living had seen Dial's face, at least not that they knew it was Dial they were looking at. The witnesses he allowed to survive saw only a linen duster, a floursack mask, and the ten-gauge bores of a Greener.

Worse than that, Dial and his men knew how to keep their mouths shut between jobs. None of them had ever been known to give themselves away by loud bragging or flashy spending. They hit, they helped themselves to whatever they wanted, and they went quietly away.

The only way a name had been attached to Dial for his crimes was the series of taunting notes that he left behind at the scenes of his robberies.

In addition to being damned good at what he did, the man who called himself Jonas Dial was a smart-ass. He enjoyed thumbing his nose at the law while he went merrily about his work.

Did the Pinkerton Agency want Jonas Dial? No question about it.

"Two thousand dollars," Raider said quickly. "It could tote up to more than that by now, but I'm sure of that much. No questions asked. Hard money, paid from my hand into yours, mister, if, but only if, this Dial is brought in."

"Dead or alive?" the little man asked nervously.

"The money gets paid either way," Raider affirmed.

"If he was ever to find out..."

"Not from me, he wouldn't."

"Dead'd be better."

"I won't give no guarantees about that. If I can take a man alive, I will. I don't hold with murder for hire."

"It's just... he'd kill me sure if he was to find out I jobbed him. You got to understand that."

"Two thousand dollars hard money," Raider said softly. "And my word that no one outside the Pinkerton Agency has to hear from me who put me onto Jonas Dial."

The man swallowed hard and glanced past Raider toward the empty main street of Chloride, Arizona.

"All right. All right, then," the fat man whispered. "Listen close, mister Pink, and I'll tell you where you can find Jonas Dial."

A slow smile tugged at the corners of Raider's mouth as he bent and listened to what this frightened tipster had to say.

CHAPTER THREE

Raider scowled and tried the doorknob. Not that it was any use. The telegraph office was dark and obviously empty, but he tried the door anyway, then accepted the inevitable and turned away.

He really needed to inform the Chicago office about what he was doing, damn it. Procedure aside, he needed to tell them that there wouldn't be an operative on hand in Chloride to meet with Phipps when the guy finally showed up.

One way or another, though, Raider was not going to miss out on this opportunity to nail Jonas Dial. Phipps and his missing daughter could just damn well wait.

According to the anonymous tipster—the man had refused to give Raider a name, insisting instead on a code arrangement in which he was known to Raider only as "the man from the Blue Walls"—Jonas Dial had been hiding out for the past several months in the Panamint mountain range near Death Valley.

Now Dial was on the move again, set to link up with

the other members of his gang at Cedar City, Utah, where their next job would be planned or perhaps executed. The tipster said he wasn't sure which.

Either way, he said, Dial was on the move. And tomorrow he was supposed to stop overnight at an abandoned stage stop known as Blue Walls.

Dial would be coming alone on this leg of the journey. His men were also scattered, with everyone set to converge at Cedar City by prearranged agreement.

Raider had been skeptical about the information and pressed the unnamed tipster about how he had gotten word about it.

"I, uh, used to have something to do with the stage station, see. Before the line went under and it was left be. It's on the old coach road. Anyhow, mister, I know that country. I, uh, was hired to meet Mr. Dial there. With a change of horses. Two horses, no saddles. I'm supposed to meet him there with the fresh mounts and take away the horses he's brought that far."

"Two horses?"

"Two. Mr. Dial, he don't trust nothing to luck, and a man afoot in that country is in for it. Country like that, he always wants a spare horse trailing along ready in case the one horse busts a leg or gets the colic or something."

Raider had raised an eyebrow at that point but hadn't brought up the obvious. The "man from the Blue Walls" seemed to know more about Jonas Dial and his habits than this simple job would require. If the tipster wasn't actually a member of Dial's gang he at least was mighty close to them.

Still, if the secret could be bought out of him for two thousand dollars it would be money well spent. And "no questions asked" had been part of the deal. Raider clamped his jaw firmly shut and asked no more on that particular subject.

"I'm to have the horses there by noon tomorrow,"

the man said. "The way I see it, Mr. Dial will want to get there sometime in the forenoon, sleep through the heat, an' then move on again come sundown when the country starts to cool off some. That's the way he likes to do it."

Again Raider concentrated on remaining silent and letting the man talk all he wanted.

"There's time enough for you to show up at the Walls 'stead of me, you see. You'd be a little past noon if you was to leave right away. But not so late that you'd scare Mr. Dial off, I wouldn't think. Travel in that country is iffy at the best. He won't be worried if I don't show right on the mark. He might spook an' run if things don't go to plan pretty quick, though. You'd best know that right up front. You fuck around and take your time getting there, there won't be nobody for you to find."

Raider had grunted and asked the tipster to lead him to the old stage station.

"No, sir. No way I'd do that. Come within fifty mile of Mr. Dial when he might get pissed at me? No, sir. I can give you directions how to get there. But I won't be riding out of here with you. Not a foot of the way, I won't. No, sir."

Even a cash bribe hadn't been able to sway him off that resolution.

And Raider had no time at all to waste in Chloride thinking about it.

Blue Walls was nearly seventy miles north in the middle of some lean, mean country.

Leaving right now would put Raider at the stage station a little past noon. *If* he was lucky and *if* he kept his horse to a killing pace throughout the night and on into tomorrow.

"You strike due north from here," the tipster said. "Cross the Colorado River—no ford there, but there's a place where the banks are easy enough an' you can swim it—an' keep to the west of the Virgins."

"Virgins?" Raider asked with a grin.

The man had no sense of humor. "Virgin Mountains," he said.

"Oh."

"Anyhow, once you get near to level with the Virgins an' them almost straight east from you, you'll cut the old wagon road. You can't miss the ruts, 'specially as by then it should be daylight. Turn east on the road and follow it to Blue Walls. You won't miss that neither, though there isn't much left of it by now."

"Why is it called Blue Walls?"

" 'Cause some idjit with no sense an' too much time to think up mischief had the walls painted blue once. Lord knows I'll never understand why, but they're sure enough blue-painted stone. Like I say, real hard to miss that."

"Yeah, I'd think so."

"You get there in time, Mr. Pink, and you'll find Mr. Dial lying down asleep waiting for his fresh horses."

Or not, Raider had thought silently to himself. If the relay man hadn't arrived, and of course he wouldn't have, a man as canny as Jonas Dial might well be wide awake and ready.

Either way, by damn, this was Raider's and the Pinkerton Agency's chance to put Dial away where he rightfully belonged.

Raider figured to do this job easy if he could or hard if he had to. But he did most definitely intend to take Jonas Dial out of circulation and keep the man from murdering any more potential witnesses against him.

"How will I know Dial?" Raider asked finally.

"Shit, man, he'll be the only guy there at the Walls. Won't be nobody with him."

"But what if somebody else just happens to be travelin' through?" Raider insisted.

"Won't be. Hasn't been anybody 'cross that road in three, four years, prob'ly."

"Mister, I ain't gonna take the chance of bringing in some innocent traveler," Raider said.

The tipster frowned and hesitated but finally relented just a little. "Mr. Dial is a small man. Looks kinda like a bank clerk. Goin' bald right here," he pulled his cap off and pointed toward the back of his head. "And he generally wears a real thin little mustache."

"You can identify him, then?"

The man looked frightened. "No way, mister. I won't testify to nothing, not even that you and me ever talked. Some law dog tries to haul me into a court, man, I don't know you an' I never heard o' no Jonas Dial. No, sir, not me."

Raider grimaced and nodded. Time enough to worry about changing the man's mind once Dial was safely locked away and could present no threat to the tipster's safety.

"I better get going," Raider said.

"Remember. You don't tell nobody, 'specially not Mr. Dial."

"I remember," Raider promised. "You sure you wouldn't guide me to Blue Walls? I'd pay you."

"No chance," the man said with a shudder. "I don't wanta be anyplace near there. You'll find it easy enough, though. Just do like I told you and you'll find Mr. Dial just like I said."

That had been ten minutes ago, and already Raider was wishing that the tipster had found him earlier in the evening. Hell, he would even have been willing to forgo the company of Nina and Nita if it would have given him a better chance at getting to this Blue Walls place in time to nab Jonas Dial.

CHAPTER FOUR

Raider was almighty glad the hotel staff was so helpful. He had a bellboy dash upstairs to gather his gear from the hotel room and bring it down while Raider settled his bill. Another bellboy hurried off to hire a pair of stout horses, the best the Chloride livery had to offer, complete with one saddle, an extra halter and picket ropes, and extra canteens.

Meanwhile Raider was busy writing out a message to be sent off to Chicago as quick as the telegraph office opened in the morning.

Normally he would have encrypted a fully explanatory message in the Pinkerton code, but he didn't want to take time enough to do that now. The process wasn't difficult, but it was certainly cumbersome. It would take him the better part of an hour to put everything he wanted to say into code, and that was time he did not intend to take here in the comfort of a hotel lobby. Not when that hour could mean the difference between catching Jonas Dial at Blue Walls or possibly missing the man.

He had to settle instead for jotting down a bare minimum of information—no sense in taking chances with Dial's name, in particular, since sympathizers or even other members of his gang could hear of it if the hotel staff or telegrapher had loose tongues—and trusting it to the desk clerk to send for him.

IMPOSSIBLE TO MEET CLIENT PHIPPS STOP WILL EXPLAIN FULLEST LATER STOP WILL CONTACT YOU SOONEST STOP SIGNED RAIDER

He wrote the message out and gave it to the friendly clerk.

"Don't you worry about a thing, Mr. Raider. I'll see this off to Chicago first thing in the morning, quick as Teddy opens his doors," the desk man promised.

Raider thanked the man and gave him a generous tip for his troubles.

He tipped the bellboys heavily also for their efforts. Allan would squawk about the amounts on Raider's expense voucher. But not very loudly if by then Jonas Dial was sitting behind bars.

"The horses you wanted are right outside, Mr. Raider, and we have your stuff all tied onto the saddle for you."

"You've been a big help, thanks."

He followed the bellboys outside and got his first look at the horses that had been hired for him.

The livery man in Chloride seemed to know his business. Both mounts, a pair of drab browns, were sleek and nicely muscled beneath their unexciting coats. They had broad chests and wide flaring nostrils that promised stamina.

Raider took a moment to readjust the way his scabbarded Winchester hung—a man didn't want his rifle dangling in an unfamiliar manner if there was a chance he might want the thing out of the scabbard and into his hand in a hurry—but everything else seemed secure enough.

"I expect to be back in three days or so," he said. "If there's any messages for me, hold them here, please."

"Yes, sir, Mr. Raider. And if Mr. Phipps asks for you?"

"Tell him somebody will be along to meet him directly."

"Yes, sir."

Raider swung onto the seat of the unfamiliar saddle and wriggled a bit to find the most comfortable posture on it, then touched the brim of his Stetson to the clerk and the bellboys who had followed him outdoors.

It was just past ten o'clock by now. And he had a helluva lot of ground to cover in the next fourteen hours.

CHAPTER FIVE

If this wasn't so damned serious, Raider would resent having to do it.

Riding a strange horse through the night over unknown terrain in search of a man who would almost certainly try to kill him once he got there—that wasn't exactly Raider's idea of a good time.

His butt hurt, his eyes burned, and he was cold to the bone from the soaking he'd gotten when he swam the Colorado.

But he was making good time. At least there was that to be said for it.

As the morning sun dried his clothes and began to warm him he almost felt better.

By taking two horses instead of just the one he was able to keep on pressing ahead without having to stop now and then.

The tried-and-true pattern followed by the cavalry, learned through years of rugged experience, was to trot most of the time, walk the mount part of the time, and dismount and lead the horse the remaining time. For a man making a forced march with only one animal available to him, that was the best method possible.

In Raider's current situation, taking his cue from Jonas Dial's experience in this country and that of the tipster from Blue Walls, he was able to keep moving forward at a good pace.

He stopped every ten miles or so, pausing just long enough to switch the saddle from one horse to the other, then resuming a steady road jog while the other horse rested by traveling without the encumbrance of a rider's weight on its back.

It seemed to be working well. Neither livery horse could be considered fresh at this point, but then neither was badly sweated either. They seemed to be bearing up better than Raider had any right to expect from rented mounts.

Already he could see the low, barren humps of rock that he took to be the Virgins. The ugly little mountains—in other parts of the country they wouldn't make much in the way of hills, much less be called mountains—were miles away on his right front quarter. But they were in sight, by damn.

He stood in the stirrups for a quarter mile or so just for the pleasure of having a change of position, and the horse he was riding at the moment moved on at a steady, fluid pace. The led horse trailed easily, with the lead rope hanging slack.

The country Raider was passing through here was everything the tipster had said and then some.

This was one rough, dry piece of ground.

Once the Colorado was left behind, so much as a clump of grass became a rare and valuable thing.

Trees? Straight ahead. Look for them about when you got to Idaho, Raider figured. But there didn't seem much sense in looking for one before then. There hadn't even been any trees along the Colorado River, the now-and-then floods apparently swept away any that tried to take root along the course of the only reliable water in more miles than a sane man wanted to walk.

Hell, even cactus was rare hereabouts. Too little water even for those.

Sand? Well, a man who got his jollies from sand would be in fine shape here. Or rock. There was plenty of rock, too.

Sand and rock and heat this country was damn well equipped to offer.

Now that the sun was fully up and his clothes completely dried, Raider decided that being cold and wet hadn't been so bad after all.

Sun like this would boil a lizard's blood. When the critter was lying in the shade.

No, this wasn't country for vacationing tourists to come to.

Raider tried to concentrate his thoughts on other things while he rode steadily forward and the Virgins came nearer bit by ever so slight bit.

He thought perversely about cold running mountain creeks and the cool heights of a snowcapped mountain. About trout pulled fresh for the frying pan and geese roasting in an oven.

Must be getting hungry, he decided, realizing where his thoughts were starting to take him.

It was bad enough that he felt like he was riding through a damned oven. Worse though, he'd forgotten to get that hotel clerk to have a lunch packed for him or road supplies laid in.

He'd remembered the canteens and water but completely forgot that his usual supply of jerky had been used up lately and not yet replenished. Damn it.

And last night's supper was a long time gone.

Since he had nothing better to do to amuse himself while he rode, he half turned in the saddle and rooted through his gear looking for a forgotten scrap of jerky or a chunk of moldy biscuit. The best he could come up with were a few dozen unground coffee beans that had been lost in the seams of his saddlebags.

He pulled one of those out and tried chewing it to see if that would help satisfy his hunger.

It didn't take long to arrive at an answer. The hard, crunchy bean was bitter and vile in his mouth. He spat the thing out and tried to wash the discomfort away with a mouthful of tepid water, but that was only marginally successful. He wished too late that he hadn't tried it.

Time to switch horses again. He slowed to a walk, then stopped and stepped down to the ground. The sun-baked earth was hard under his boots.

He switched the bridle first, then unstrapped the cinches and dumped the saddle onto the ground. He pulled the blanket out from under it and snapped it to dislodge any clinging hair. There wasn't time enough to let the sweaty blanket dry, but at least he could refold it to present a relatively clean and dry surface. He took special pains to smooth the blanket over the back of the fresher horse. A crease or wrinkle underneath the bars of a saddle can lead to galls, and a sore-backed horse wasn't much use.

Finally, satisfied, Raider snugged his cinches again and swung back into the saddle.

Damn, it had felt good to stand up and move around a bit there.

Still, the Virgins were almost due east from him now. And the sun was climbing high. He should soon hit the old stage road the man from Blue Walls had told him about.

Then it would be a race to see if he could get to the abandoned station before Jonas Dial pulled out or, barring that, catch up with the son of a bitch before Dial reached Cedar City and disappeared among the locals and the perfectly innocent and legitimate travelers who might be found there.

Raider stifled a yawn that might've broken his jaw if he'd let it gather a full head of steam and bumped the horse into the accustomed jog again.

CHAPTER 6

Raider frowned and cussed just a little and pulled the horses down to a walk for the final approach to the Blue Walls.

Just like the tipster had said, he had no trouble identifying the place.

The old stage stop was built of native rock laid up with a haphazard mud mortar. A primary building where the station keeper must have lived and served meals for the passengers going through. A single outhouse behind the main building. A half-walled storage building. And a low, stone corral wall that hadn't had the benefit of any mortar and so was falling apart now after a period of neglect.

Somebody, for some obscure reason, had taken a notion to paint everything standing except for the corral walls a startling shade of blue. The paint was flaked and fading now, but even so it jarred the eye in this brown and barren country.

No chance at all that there was some *other* place in

this country that would be called Blue Walls.

This was definitely it.

Unfortunately, "it" was definitely empty.

Far as Raider could tell as he slowly approached the old stage station, he might be the only live human within a hundred miles or more, and the horses he was riding the only other live creatures in as great a distance.

The corral was standing empty, and there was no hint of life to be seen anywhere around the Blue Walls.

He cussed again, more forcefully this time, and reached down to make sure the Remington was riding loose in his holster. Just in case. Raider had been mistaken about something once. Back one time when he thought he'd made an error and then was proven wrong about that. It wouldn't much do to make a mistake about Blue Walls being deserted and let Jonas Dial nail him.

He glanced toward the cloudless sky. The sun wasn't quite yet at its zenith. He'd made better time than he'd expected thanks to the relay of horses. Hell, maybe he'd managed to get here ahead of Dial.

So much the better if it would be Raider who had the advantage of rock walls to stand behind when Dial showed.

And there could be half a hundred reasons why Dial might come in late. One of his horses could've gone lame on him and he had to come on with just one mount. He might just've overslept this morning. Any number of reasons. Whatever, if he was here first, Raider would be pleased.

He circled wide so he could ride in with the corral between him and the station house. Just in case. If an eyeball or a rifle muzzle appeared at one of those windows, it would be nice to have something solid to drop behind.

He needn't have worried, though.

Not only was the corral empty, there were no manure piles to indicate that any horses had been here recently.

Raider was definitely here ahead of Jonas Dial.

The only traces of manure he could see were some darker brown patches of dust on the corral floor to show where old manure piles had long ago dried out and started blowing away.

There hadn't been a horse here in months, maybe in years.

Even then Raider didn't let down his caution. He ground-tied his horses inside the corral and slid the Winchester out of the scabbard, then made a slow approach to the stationhouse on foot.

The place was empty as a whore's conscience.

The walls still stood, but most of the roof was gone, and there wasn't anything left inside to show where furniture might have been.

Four flat stones set deep into the earth toward the rear of the building showed where the iron feet of a stove or range might once have stood.

Some pieces of framing timber indicated where a partition would have been, probably covered with canvas or blanketing instead of valuable lumber, to divide the building into one large room and one small one. The small one, Raider guessed, would have been the station keeper's living quarters and the big one the public room.

But there wasn't any hint that anyone had been here since the day the Blue Walls were abandoned.

Just to be on the safe side, Raider investigated the shed and the outhouse, too.

The shed was empty except for the fallen remains of its roof. The outhouse still had some dry, aged poles in place for a seat, and a catalog containing a few dozen yellowed, curling pages hung handy on a peg wedged between two of the wall stones. The place had been out of use so long there wasn't even any smell from it anymore.

Raider sighed and tried to relax.

DESERT DEATH TRAP 33

He was kind of hoping, though, that Jonas Dial would hurry up and get here.

Raider was counting on the foresighted Dial to be carrying a good supply of food with him. Right now that would be almost as welcome as getting the cuffs onto Dial's wrists.

Not that wishing for things made them happen real often.

Raider walked back over to the corral and unsaddled the horse he'd been riding the last leg of the way, then gave both animals a brisk rubdown and turned them loose to roll in the dust and dry themselves off.

He dropped the saddle on top of the crumbling wall—Dial would be expecting to see two horses and one man's gear when he rode in—retrieved his Winchester, and went back to the station-house to wait for the arrival of the guest of honor.

Everything so far seemed to be going much better than he might have hoped.

CHAPTER SEVEN

The son of a bitch was certainly taking his time. It was coming dusk, and Jonas Dial was many hours overdue. Almost as bad, the hunger pains in Raider's stomach kept gnawing and nagging at him.

If something had happened to change Dial's plans, would the tipster with the horse relay have been notified?

Possibly not, Raider conceded. The greedy little man was no heavy player in Dial's gang. Couldn't be. A man like Dial wouldn't think a lightweight like that worth worrying over.

On the other hand . . .

Hell, a man could go round the bend trying to fret through all the possibilities of a situation like this.

The best thing was to sit tight and wait for Dial to either show or not.

If he showed, fine. Raider would take him and be done with it. If not—by noon tomorrow, say—he would ride back to Chloride and no harm done except to Allan Pinkerton's blood pressure over Raider not being where he was supposed to be when Phipps finally put in an appearance.

Allan could stand an increase in his heart rate. Be good for him to get the circulation flowing.

Raider grunted and tried to ignore the steady pangs of discomfort in his belly.

It was getting cold, too, now that the sun was down, but he didn't want to light a fire.

It would have done no harm to show a light, of course. After all, Dial was expecting to find someone waiting for him at the Blue Walls. The danger would have been that then Raider's night vision would be ruined while Dial, approaching the old station in the night, had an advantage.

With a man like Dial you don't want to give anything away if you can help it.

Raider frowned and made do.

After it was full dark he picked up the Winchester that had been leaning against the doorjamb all these useless hours and stepped outside.

If he couldn't have anything to eat, he could at least fill his gut with water to take away some of the hunger. Besides, the horses would need water too by now.

There should be a well somewhere near, of course.

Though come to think of it he couldn't recall noticing it earlier.

He shrugged. A man tends to overlook the ordinary.

He paused outside the abandoned station and inspected the full sweep of the horizon, listening as much as looking for signs of movement. Dial could come in from any point of the compass regardless of the direction he was traveling in, just as Raider had made a circle before approaching the station himself. And Raider didn't want to be caught flat-footed if Dial chose this moment to show.

As far as Raider could tell there wasn't so much as a coyote moving for miles around.

He went on out to the corral, speaking in a soft, soothing voice as he did so, so the horses wouldn't be spooked by his approach.

The horses were probably as hungry and worn out as he was, because there was no sound from them in response. Sleeping, he guessed, which was a luxury he wouldn't be able to give himself until the business with Dial was resolved.

He reached the crumbling wall and carefully searched the countryside all around again before he slipped over the wall and into the corral.

Both horses were lying down, he saw by the thin starlight. Both of them over at the back of the corral.

He skirted a pile of fresh manure that was dark against the pale, hard-baked ground and crooned under his breath again as he moved toward the horses.

Neither of the animals responded.

Raider felt a cold chill shoot through him like ice.

He dropped into a crouch, his hand sweeping the Remington out without conscious thought.

There was . . . nothing.

Nothing to see. Nothing to hear. For damn sure nothing to shoot at.

But this didn't feel right all of a sudden.

Keeping low, Raider crabbed forward to the nearer dark shape that was one of his horses.

He knelt beside the animal and touched its neck.

The horse didn't move.

"Oh, shit," he muttered aloud.

He poked the animal's hide.

He was pushing on limp meat.

The horse was dead.

The flesh under his palm was warm. The animal had died recently. And almighty quiet.

Raider leaned forward. He could smell the faint, coppery scent of fresh blood in the air.

A dark stain on the earth beneath the horse's throat

showed that the thing had bled plenty. Been bled to death maybe for it to die so quiet that Raider hadn't been able to hear even when his senses were keyed to a sharp pitch in anticipation of Dial coming in.

But how . . . ?

He moved sideways and low, revolver still at the ready, to the other horse.

It too was freshly killed, a dark gleam of blood under its throat and not yet sunken into the crust of the earth reflecting the pinpoints of light from the stars high above.

But who . . . ?

Raider stood, his face a mask of cold anger, and strained to make out any faint sound or motion from the arid, empty land around the Blue Walls.

There was nothing. Not so much as a whiff of breeze to rattle what little brush there was here.

*Some*one had damn sure come in and killed these horses.

The animals hadn't gone and committed suicide by slitting their own throats.

But who, damn it? And why?

Jonas Dial?

That made no sense. It wasn't a Pinkerton operative Dial was expecting here.

Besides, Raider would be willing to swear that no horseman had come within two miles of the station since Raider got here. And none for months before him either.

Someone, then, who had a hard-on for Dial and killed the horses thinking to get back at the master criminal but instead stranding Raider here by mistake?

That held no more logic than the first thought had.

Yet someone had damn sure managed to slide in quiet as a ghost in the night and just as silently put both horses down.

Someone who was damned good at moving in the dark for him to get this job done and Raider not know about it.

Raider frowned and retreated the way he had just come. Standing out here in the corral wasn't going to bring those horses back to life. The protection of blue-painted stone walls around him wouldn't be bad to have right now.

He angled off to the side a little, stepped over a low spot in the corral wall, and shifted sideways to the place where his saddle and gear hung.

His spare ammunition was in his saddlebags. And he was beginning to get the idea that he just might be wanting that close to hand.

He reached for the saddlebags.

And came up with nothing but the cantle of the rented saddle.

The saddlebags were gone. So was everything else Raider had left on the worn saddle.

Except, oddly, his canteens.

Both of them were where he'd slung them, one riding on either side of the horn.

He slipped the strap of one off the horn and lifted it.

The canteen came up light and easy in his hand.

There was no weight of water to be lifted with it.

Raider felt a stab of sudden concern.

He grabbed the second canteen, but it too was light and completely empty.

A brief touch told him why. There was a thin hole stabbed through the bottom of each cloth-covered tin canteen. And each of those holes was what you would expect from a sturdy knife blade being shoved into the metal.

The insulating cloth that was glued to the outside of each canteen was wet and chill around the knife punctures.

Just as with the still warm bodies of the horses, this had been done almighty recently.

Dry as this country was and quick as water will evaporate, the canteens couldn't have been holed any longer ago than ten minutes. Fifteen minutes tops.

Since dark fell, then.

And they did it while Raider was standing in that doorway over there not thirty yards distant, watching and listening for all he was worth.

What the *hell* was this about?

He swallowed, his hunger forgotten now but his throat feeling suddenly dry with the knowledge that he had no canteens of water to turn to, and moved fast toward the Blue Walls.

CHAPTER EIGHT

Jonas Dial never came.

Raider waited the long night through, but there was no sign of Dial or of any other human. Coyotes laughed and chattered in the distance, and bats or night-flying birds fluttered around the eaves of the tumbledown way station. But no one and nothing else moved.

By dawn Raider was near exhaustion. He had spent the night just past waiting for the unseen, unknown horse killers and canteen emptiers to make a move against him. There had been nothing. But he hadn't known he could rely on that. He had had to sit with the Winchester in his hands and his senses attuned to the slightest noise or movement the whole night long.

The night before that he had spent in the saddle racing to get here ahead of Jonas Dial. He hadn't slept in . . . he was too groggy and disoriented at the moment to work out just how long it had been.

Too damned long. He was sure about that.

His throat and eyes felt like they had been packed with

desert sand, and a fog of fatigue dulled his mind.

He stood, nearly lost his balance, and had to grab hold of the blue-painted stone wall for support to keep himself from going to his knees.

Lordy! What the hell was going on here?

The early light slanted down onto the barren landscape, illuminating the lumpy peaks of the Virgins and making them seem all the more arid and forbidding, then streaking on to reach the jarring blue of the Blue Walls and the drab, ochre brown of the dry, dusty country that spread flat and empty for miles around.

Raider shivered as a chill ran up his spine. Then he stepped out into the new daylight.

Mushy and dull though his mental processes were at this point, he was nonetheless thinking, planning, working out how best to cope with the situation.

The first thing would be to find the well that had served the men and the remounts at the Blue Walls. That need was so obvious it required no thought.

First find the well and drink. Then sleep. Then patch the canteens somehow—he would be able to work that out easily enough once he was rested and had a bellyful of water—and prepare to walk out.

The Colorado was—what? Forty miles south? No matter. However far it was, that was how far he would have to walk with the canteens. Refill them there easily enough. Cross to the Arizona side . . . or was it Utah at that point? For some reason he insisted on dwelling on that inconsequential detail and had to force himself to concentrate on matters of importance instead . . . and continue down to Chloride again.

Chloride was the nearest point he was sure of.

Cedar City might be closer. Or . . . or . . . what the hell was there along the road in the other direction? The tipster had said, hadn't he? Or had he? Raider couldn't remember right now. Something in Nevada, anyway. Death Valley? Was there anything closer than Death Valley?

Tonopah? Shit, he couldn't remember how to scratch his own ass at the moment. Couldn't concentrate. He needed sleep. Water first. Then sleep.

He walked weak-kneed and swaying out into the early sunlight and looked around.

There was still no hint of color or motion that would show him who it was who was trying to do this to him. Who it was who had killed those horses and holed his canteens. Sons of bitches. Whoever they were they were sons of bitches.

The Winchester felt heavy and unresponsive in his hands. He lugged it with him anyway.

The corral was as he had left it except for some tiny footprints left in the dust. Small rodents had already discovered the dead horses and begun the job of cleaning up the carrion. Today the birds would come.

The saddle hung undisturbed on the stone corral wall.

The picket ropes were gone, though, Raider noticed, and the horses' halters had been removed. Whoever had killed the animals must have wanted those. But why not simply steal the horses and all the gear and be done with it?

It wasn't worth trying to think about right now.

Right now Raider needed to find that damned well. Then try to get some sleep.

Lordy, he needed sleep. Forty-eight hours of it would be just about right. For starters.

He leaned against the corral wall and squinted, trying to ease the burning in his eyes and to find the damned well. There had to be a well. You couldn't have a way station without a well.

He could see the station building, of course. And the shed. And the outhouse. And the corral.

Nothing else. Absolutely nothing else except dry ground and pale sky.

There had to be a fucking well around here someplace.
Had to be.

Just because he couldn't see one right this second didn't mean that there wasn't one.

He laid the forestock of the Winchester over his shoulder and began a slow, methodical search for the lousy missing water well.

He started at the Blue Walls themselves and began making slow, thorough circles around and around the lousy place.

It wasn't easy trying to keep his circles rounded and even.

It occurred to him after a while that he was concentrating more on walking in nice, even circles than he was in looking for the damn well.

For some reason it seemed important to make the circles regular and tidy.

Jeez, he needed rest.

But he needed water first.

First the well. Then the sleep.

He tried to keep his thoughts focused on that single point of looking for the well that had to be here. Someplace.

He stumbled over a greasewood root that had been half grubbed out of the hard earth, nearly went to his knees, but righted himself in time and managed to keep his feet.

He squinted again and stared.

The station and all the buildings were seventy-five, a hundred yards away. He was wandering around in the middle of the fucking brush. What little of it there was.

Wasn't anywhere near the Blue Walls now.

Not near enough, anyway, that they would have dug a damn well all the way out here.

A man doesn't want to lug buckets of water all that distance.

Country like this you get your well in first, then you put the buildings close to the water. You don't trust trying to do it the other damn way around.

So why hadn't he found the lousy well yet?

He stopped, shuddered, shook his head vigorously from side to side, trying to clear the spiderwebs from his brain.

There had to be a well here someplace.

He'd been so lost in trying to concentrate on walking in neat circles that he must have walked right past the damn thing and never noticed.

Stupid damn thing for a man to do, Raider chided himself.

Real stupid.

He grimaced and tried to spit, but his mouth felt like it was full of cotton, and he couldn't work up any spit to get the bad taste out.

How long had it been since he'd had anything to drink? Yesterday morning sometime? About that. Had to be a damn well around here someplace.

Stubbornly, Raider went back to the front of the station building, set the Winchester carefully against the blue stone wall, and began once more to make his slow, careful, increasingly larger circles.

This time he concentrated every moment on looking for that son of a bitch well.

Before he was half done, though, he felt a chill lying on his shoulders in spite of the heat of the late morning sun.

There was no water well at the Blue Walls.

CHAPTER NINE

Raider felt better when he woke up. Marginally, but better. His tongue still felt like it had been hung out on a line to dry, but at least he wasn't so foggy and slow in the thinking department anymore.

It was dusk by then, and only the slightly paler sky off to the west informed him that the sun was sinking and not coming up again. He had slept so soundly that it might have gone either way.

There still was no sign of whoever it was who had killed the horses and, much worse, holed the canteens.

And that still made no damn sense to him.

Why anyone should go to that kind of trouble and then not follow up on it...

He could fret about things like that later. Right now there were other things that needed doing.

The first of those, of course, was to make another search around the Blue Walls for that missing well.

Surely there had to be one. It was not impossible that in his earlier groggy state he might simply have missed seeing it. If it was underneath the fallen shed roof, say, for instance if the shed hadn't been for storage purposes but was there to protect an open well against evaporation loss or . . . Anyway, he would look. That was what it came down to. He would look again there and everywhere else he could think of.

He came to his feet, aching a little in his joints but otherwise not in bad shape, and ventured out of the station building.

No one shot at him. Nothing in the distance moved. Closer in there was a panicked fluttering of wings, and a flock of ugly black carrion eaters lifted heavily out of the corral enclosure at his approach. Flies buzzed and droned busily as they demanded their share of the blood and horse meat.

Raider glanced in that direction but didn't bother going any closer. There was nothing there that he wanted to see. Now.

Damn shame that it had taken him so long to realize the full extent of his predicament, though. If he'd known soon enough he could have bled the horses and gotten some moisture from their blood. Now it was much too late for that or for claiming any meat from the carcasses. A long night and a sunny day would have coagulated the blood and rendered the meat unfit for use. Pity.

He checked inside the shed again, but all he found under the tumbledown roof was a dirt floor and a few bent horseshoe nails.

So much for that idea.

While he still had a little light left he made another circuit of the ground around the old station. This time, feeling sharper and better able to think clearly, he spotted several places where someone had tried to dig in the far distant past.

No well, but perhaps where someone once tried to locate water.

Had the stage line hauled water out here, then? If so

it would have been from sheer necessity, but it wasn't impossible. A mail contract to meet, perhaps, and a relay station required to do it. The expense and the trouble would have been high. But it wasn't impossible that each coach could have brought a barrel or two of water along to leave here or that a tank wagon had been used. Raider had seen some water trailers used at Army posts, available for extended dry marches. General Crook had used such to supply his heliograph stations during the Apache wars, Raider thought. Or had that been someone else? He couldn't recall at the moment. Maybe he wasn't thinking quite so clearly as he'd hoped.

He sighed and looked some more, but daylight and hope deserted him at about the same time.

There really wasn't any water at the Blue Walls.

He cleared his throat—no easy task, dry as it was—and went back to the stationhouse.

He sat on the hard ground with his back against the sun-warmed stone wall and tried to work this through.

If the rest of his gear hadn't been taken, this wouldn't have been quite so bad. Bad but not awful. A man can take seemingly dry desert foliage and crush it, pack it inside a rubberized slicker, and put the bundle out in the bright sunlight. The heat from the sun will steam out whatever moisture is in the plants, and the rubberized surface will keep the bit of artificial dew from evaporating. You can't manufacture much in the way of water that way, but any little bit would be damned welcome at this point.

Unfortunately, Raider's slicker was gone too. Taken off his saddle when those canteens were deliberately ruined and left for him to find.

Could be that somebody else knew about that trick with a slicker then.

He frowned and without thinking touched the worn grips of his Remington.

If that was what was happening here, then the silent attack was deliberate.

The whole thing? Could it *all* be part of some deliberate plan that he couldn't begin to figure out?

Jonas Dial hadn't showed up when and where he was supposed to. Had this been some kind of misdirection orchestrated by Dial and his gang?

Could Dial have learned that there was a Pinkerton operative in Chloride—it wasn't like that was any great secret, after all; the tipster had certainly heard about him being there—and *arranged* for Raider to be here without horses or water?

That could make a left-handed sort of sense. If, say, Dial and his boys were planning something in Chloride. If Raider's accidental presence there might have gotten in their way. If . . . He sighed. *If* covered just too damn much ground.

The only thing he was sure of was that he wasn't going to sort out any of it while he was sitting here in the middle of noplace waiting to dry out and die of thirst.

He *had* to have water.

And he had to get the hell away from here.

No one visited the Blue Walls anymore. Not for months, maybe years on end. Raider had seen that for himself by the absence of manure piles in the corral when he got here.

He damn sure couldn't count on someone riding to his rescue by a whim of chance.

If Raider expected to get back to Chloride with a whole skin, he was going to have to count on himself to get the job done.

Only himself.

And he wasn't very damn likely to get that done by sitting on his butt and waiting for inspiration to strike.

Better to start walking now while he still had some strength left and no sun-heat to contend with.

But first things first.

He stood, very much aware that his strength had already dropped off to an alarming degree, and walked over to the corral wall. He had no need for a canteen right now, but he might well need one later. He would carry one of the empties, he decided. Two empty canteens would be a burden, but one that was empty now but capable of being filled at some point in the future could be a lifesaver. A real one.

He looked both of them over, but there was very little light now to see by. The stars were fine for giving direction, but they made damn poor lamps.

He chose the canteen that had the larger hole in it and discarded the other. Even though there was a bigger puncture in the one he would keep, the edges of the cut were smooth and even, and the width of the hole was quite regular.

The saddle would have to be abandoned here. Trying to carry it with him would be foolish.

The thing wasn't useless, though.

He flipped it over onto the hard seat and examined the leathers.

The material was much too thick and hard-tanned to be of any use.

He cut the strings off and stuffed them into a pocket. Leather thongs might come in handy to make snares if he had to stop for any extended period of time.

There was a sheepskin pad glued to the underside of the saddle. Raider used his belt knife to cut that away and expose the padding that lay underneath the saddle tree, supposed to protect a horse's back from abrasion by the bars of the tree.

A layer of woolen batting was of no interest to him, but the sheet of thin leather that lay between it and the rawhide-wrapped wooden tree certainly was.

He chopped out a palm-sized piece of the soft, thin, flexible leather and trimmed that into a narrow strip that was just about the same width as the puncture hole in the bottom of the canteen, then cut that down again to a piece only a couple of inches long.

Doubled over and stuffed inside the hole, it should serve as a stopper. Not perfect, of course, but serviceable. The canteen would leak some, but not so much, especially once he had something to put inside and the wet leather swelled.

Raider smiled for the first time in quite a while.

He needed something—any sort of makeshift tool would do—to force the folded leather into the hole in the metal canteen body.

His knife wouldn't work, of course. That would puncture the leather and ruin the purpose of it. He smiled again. The flat head of one of those discarded horseshoe nails he'd seen inside the shed would be just about right for size and strength both.

He took his canteen and leather plug and went across the station yard to the shed. It was full dark by now, so he had to get down on hands and knees and paw through the rubble on the shed floor, but he finally located a nail.

A few seconds' work and a push or two and he had a canteen that was usable once more, the leather wadding jammed firm inside the hole that had been gouged into the canteen.

Raider grunted and went outside again with the canteen slung over his shoulder.

He was about as ready to travel as he was going to get.

He angled off toward the station building to retrieve the Winchester, already searching the stars for the bearings that would take him south toward the Colorado.

Straight down, he decided. Straight for the river and its lifesaving water.

Coming up he'd had to find the old road and follow it in to locate the Blue Walls. Going back would be easier. It would be damn near impossible to miss finding the Colorado River from here. All he had to do was hoof it south until his boots felt wet. Raider figured he could handle that.

He reached the door to the Blue Walls station and reached inside for the barrel of the Winchester he'd left leaning up against the jamb.

He frowned.

His hand came up empty.

Surely the rifle hadn't fallen over. He would have heard the clatter. Besides, he'd put it there with considerable care to see that it wouldn't fall over. A man wants to take some care with his tools, whether they be firearms or ripsaws. And a front sight knocked askew in an accidental drop can be worse than embarrassing. It can be downright fatal.

Raider stepped inside the building and looked again. This time he got down on his hands and knees and felt of the ground like he'd done when he was looking for that nail.

Nothing!

He came up empty-handed.

The Winchester was gone.

It had been right there when he woke up.

He distinctly remembered that it had.

So where . . . ?

He felt a chill.

Someone had slipped in and taken the Winchester.

How? How could *any* son of a bitch have been that quiet?

They . . . he must have done it, damn it, while he was over at the corral fussing with the saddle or maybe while he was in the shed looking for that damn nail. More likely when he was in the shed, then. Surely nobody, no-damn-body could move so slick as to reach the building while Raider was standing in plain sight not thirty, forty yards away.

But then ten minutes ago he would have sworn that nobody could have gotten to the Winchester while Raider was awake and alert and inside that shed either.

He scowled.

Almost nobody.

This guy, whoever the SOB was and whatever it was that he wanted, was almighty good.

Raider fingered the Remington that still rested where it was supposed to and stared out into the night.

He shivered again, although the night was not particularly cold.

Stubbornly, and mad as hell now too, he stepped outside and began walking toward the south.

CHAPTER TEN

How long does it take a man to walk forty miles in rough country in the dark?

How long does it take for a man to keel over from lack of water?

Raider didn't have the answers to either of those questions. And the two of them sure as hell had to be looked at as separate parts of the same big question.

He grunted softly to himself and decided that the answers really didn't much matter anyhow.

The point was, he was *going* to walk down to the Colorado, and the hell with all the nitpicky little details.

One small point in favor of walking through this country: there wasn't much in the way of underbrush to stumble through. One point against it: it was damned well blessed with rocks and lumps of hard-baked soil for a man to trip over.

That kind of cross country walking is more difficult than it looks. It saps a man's strength.

That didn't matter either.

If he had to fucking crawl the forty miles to the river, Raider intended to get there and anyplace else he had to go.

He was *not* going to roll over and quit.

He walked the first mile and counted it down in his mind. Only thirty-nine to go. A whole mile less than there had been.

He kept his pace smooth and steady or at least as much so as the rugged, choppy ground permitted. Not hurrying but not lagging either. Just smooth and steady. That was what it needed.

Take the direction from the stars and move along one pace at a time.

Enough steady strides and there would be the river.

Damn, his mouth was dry.

Time to think about that when he was sitting with his feet in the river. Not now. Now just think about humping it along smooth and steady.

He judged he'd made a second mile and paused to look back over his shoulder, checking the North Star just to be sure of his bearings. That needed to become a habit. Later on he might not be thinking so clear. That was when it would be all the more important that he not veer off his path. Wobbly side steps would make the trek that much longer. Angle back and forth like a boat tacking against the wind and it could make things just enough harder that it wouldn't get done at all. So start now. Make it a solid habit to keep to the straight southward line. Don't leave anything to chance.

The North Star sneered back at him, cold and distant and aloof. But at least the little SOB was where it was supposed to be.

Beneath it there was no sign now of the Blue Walls. The drab and lonesome little way station to nowhere lay lost in the shadows of the desert.

Raider wished . . .

He clamped down hard on that kind of thinking. Wishing was dumb. Doing was all that counted. Wishing was just another form of wandering in circles.

He adjusted the strap of the empty canteen, dropping it lower so it wouldn't cut into his chest.

Then he started forward again.

Two miles behind and a mere thirty-eight to go. Then he could take a bath. Lay around a bit and have a . . .

Firelight winked on the dark, empty desert in front of him, and Raider dropped belly down onto a sharp rock.

The breath was driven out of him, but at the moment he didn't much give a shit about that.

The rifle slug hit the ground twenty yards or more in front of him and went whining and snarling off into the distance behind.

Raider's Remington was in his hand.

But he had no damn target.

The rifle had been fired from a good three hundred yards away, and Raider might as well save a bullet and spit at the son of a bitch instead of shooting. One would do about as much good as the other. At this range a revolver is useless. Hell, even a good rifle firing at three hundreds yards or more in the dark is just about useless.

He rolled off the rock that was poking into his gut, but he didn't stand again.

The gunman was out in front of him.

Somewhere.

Blocking Raider's way to the Colorado River and safety.

Who, damn it?

And why?

The most aggravating thought of them all was that that bastard out there might well be using Raider's own Winchester to shoot at him now.

Deliberately shooting at him from an impossible distance . . . was there a reason for that, too?

If indeed it was the same guy who'd been back at the Blue Walls, he was good enough and plenty more to have gotten practically in Raider's face before he fired.

He could have gotten close enough to be sure of a killing shot before he pulled the trigger.

So why the hell hadn't he?

Why this way?

Was this some kind of insane game the son of a bitch was playing, with him the cat and Raider the mouse?

That, damn it, was insulting.

Did he want Raider to charge him? Use up his energy in useless sprints across the desert? Scare him and wear him down and make sure he couldn't get to the river?

Raider grunted. He wasn't so damned easy to scare, and he wasn't planning on turning stupid real soon. In particular he wasn't going to go leaping and bounding through the night without a purpose, burning up his energy and sweating away his body fluids without any result to show for it.

He shoved the Remington back into its holster and lay still, studying the bleak and ugly country that lay between him and the rifleman and wondering just what in hell was going to come next.

All in all, he decided, maybe he should've stayed in that bed in Chloride snuggled in between Nina and Nita.

CHAPTER ELEVEN

It was coming dawn, and Raider wasn't a step closer to the Colorado than he had been when that first shot was fired in the night.

He lay behind yet another chunk of pale, jagged rock and peered over it at the flat, barren, not-quite-empty-enough country that lay between him and the only sure source of water he knew of in this forsaken and forbidding country.

Four times during the night he had tried to slip around the unknown ambusher. Four times he hadn't gone five feet from his hiding place before the sharp-eyed son of a bitch spotted him and drove him back to cover again with a well-placed shot.

The bullets had to be well placed, damn it, because they always landed exactly the same. Close enough. But never, ever actually harmful.

They were warning shots. Nothing more, nothing less. The lead slugs told him he wasn't going south. But he wasn't going to be shot in the night either.

It was damned well maddening was what it was.

A man of *his* experience was being herded and played with like some damn greenhorn.

Twice during the night Raider had tried to worm his way backward and to the side, away from the vigilant and watchful eyes of the bastard with the rifle.

Those hadn't been any more successful than the frontal sneaks.

Each time he was spotted before he could move twenty yards.

Each time there was a bullet out of the darkness but striking behind him rather than in front.

The message was plain.

He couldn't go forward, and he couldn't go back either.

He was pinned right here where he damned well was. Getting hungrier and thirstier with every passing minute.

And that SOB out there could take him any time he wanted.

Raider still hadn't so much as seen the distant ambusher. Not a glimpse. Not a flicker. Not a hint. Nothing.

Nobody had the right to be that good. Nobody.

But this guy was.

Raider frowned and rubbed at his eyes. They felt dry and a bit painful. Already his body was trying to conserve moisture, withdrawing the fluids from his mouth and nose and eyes and hoarding what little it had left.

He wasn't particularly tired, though. At least there was that to be grateful for. Since he hadn't been able to do anything else last night he at least had managed to get some sleep. As far as the threat of the gunman out there was concerned, well, he just hadn't bothered to worry about it while he slept. There would've been no point in that. If the rifleman had wanted to kill him, Raider would be dead by now. Plain and simple. The gunman was trying to herd him, not hurt him. Trying to *tell* him something. But not just come in and kill him.

This was . . . weird.

He frowned again, said the hell with it, and stood upright as the first flow of yellow-gold light spilled around the Virgins and reached the desert floor.

Now that there was daylight in the sky, the rifleman could see him even better than before. Lying in hiding and waiting to die of thirst was no more attractive a thought than dying from a bullet would be.

Raider figured that if he could move around a bit it would force the unseen ambusher to move too. He just might get a first look at this guy who seemed to know and to control him so very, very well already.

The shots during the night had proven that he wasn't supposed to move south toward the Colorado nor back toward the Blue Walls either.

Fine. If he couldn't go north or south, he would try a few steps east or west and see what kind of reaction that drew from the ambusher.

There was no shooting now that he was on his feet.

No sign of the SOB with the rifle either. The desert in front of him might have been utterly empty for the next hundred miles for all Raider could see out there.

East or west?

East, he decided. The Virgin Mountains were in that direction. Wherever there was a dramatic change in the surface of the land there might well be surface water as well. It wasn't guaranteed in country like this—or even very dang likely, for that matter—but it was at least possible.

He would head toward the Virgins and just kinda see what happened next.

He took a few tentative steps toward the east, slowed, stepped out more quickly again.

No one shot at him.

And nothing moved to travel along with him.

At least nothing that he could *see*. He supposed it

didn't necessarily follow that nothing was moving. Only that he couldn't see anyone.

A small bird of some sort fluttered out of a cactus clump a quarter mile or so to the southeast from where Raider was.

Was the bird frightened into movement by the rifleman? Or was the thing just taking off in search of breakfast? Raider had no way to tell which it might be. If either.

He shuddered, not liking any of this worth a shit, and continued his slow hike toward the Virgins.

No one fired at or near him. No one shouted. No one showed himself.

Raider might as well have been the only human creature this side of Chloride.

He angled a bit to the south now. Then veered a little more to the south so that now he was walking toward a point well south of the lumpy Virgins. The Colorado River had to be somewhere in that general direction, even if the route to it this way would be indirect and painfully long.

From off to his right there was a puff of white smoke at the base of a ratty and ragged little clump of dusty sage.

A moment later dirt and gravel flew up from the earth twenty yards or so southeast of where Raider stood, and a moment after that he could hear the hollow bark of the gunshot.

Raider waved an acknowledgment of the warning and changed direction again, walking in a direct line toward the Virgins once more.

The gunshot was not repeated.

Apparently it was all right for him to go east. The rifleman didn't mind.

Interesting.

Raider stopped and concentrated on staring at the bit of sage where the telltale muzzle smoke had just been.

He could see ... not a damn thing.

This guy was unbelievably good.

He shrugged, shook his head, and held both hands palm upward for the rifleman to see, signifying that Raider couldn't see him, telling the bastard that Raider appreciated just how very good he was.

If you can't lick the son of a bitch, smile at him.

Raider walked on toward the dry and distant Virgin Mountains.

CHAPTER TWELVE

There's an old wives' tale, often repeated in the sort of wildly imaginative dime novel that made heroes out of some perfectly ordinary fellas, that claims a man can assuage serious thirst by carrying a pebble in his mouth.

Bullshit.

There'd been a time, back when Raider was considerably younger and more gullible than he liked to admit now, when he'd actually believed that sort of crap himself.

He'd even gone and tried that trick one time when he thought he was thirsty.

All he got out of the experience was a vile and gritty feel in his mouth and a flavor that made him think he'd picked up a pebble that a cur or a coyote had visited before him. It had cost him more moisture trying to spit out the sand and the taste than he ever could have worked up.

Besides, when you thought about it, that whole idea was stupid to begin with. It couldn't add any moisture to what you were already carrying in your body. Even if the trick worked like it was supposed to, all it could accomplish would be to make you salivate so you could swallow your own spit again.

And the thing that was needed here wasn't the comfort of thinking you had some wet stuff reaching your belly; it was a matter of genuine survival for him to add more moisture into his body.

Raider was quite willing to be uncomfortable as hell if only he could work out a way to get through this.

Dry and woody sage wasn't going to help him do that, but every now and then there was some runty, low-growing cactus spotting the desert floor.

He began zigzagging back and forth enough to reach every bit of that he came to.

Again, fortunately, the rifleman didn't seem to mind.

Every chance he got, Raider would stop long enough to kick a bulbous, spiky bit of pale cactus off its root base and use his knife to split the thing open, no matter how damn small it was.

He scooped out the bitter, pulpy interior of the plant, discarding the leathery outer skin with the spines attached, and popped the pulp into his mouth.

Even if the obnoxious stuff was no larger than a lima bean he would studiously chew on it until he reached the next clump and start over with a fresh chaw.

A proper—and wet—barrel cactus with its moist, sweet insides would have been just the ticket. But there didn't happen to be any of those around. He did the next best thing and tried to suck moisture out of every damn thing he stumbled across.

He didn't know if it was doing much good yet, but it didn't seem to be hurting anything.

The rifleman obviously could see what he was doing but didn't seem to care.

Raider hoped like hell that that didn't mean the rifleman knew something that he didn't. Like for instance that these particular varieties of cactus were poisonous or something.

Thinking about that possibility was enough to give Raider a bellyache. But he didn't quit trying to extract moisture from what was handy.

He walked on, feeling steadier now, although whether that was because he was actually getting some benefit from the cactus pulp or only because he *thought* he was, and made slow but steady progress toward the Virgins.

Once the sun climbed over the topmost ridge he had to tug the brim of his hat low to keep it out of his eyes. He hoped to hell the rifleman didn't have a hat. Serve the son of a bitch right to be annoyed by walking into the sun.

Assuming the guy was still keeping up. Raider *still* hadn't spotted him.

It had been—he squinted toward the sun—two hours or so now? About that, he decided.

Maybe the guy had dropped off back there someplace.

He tested the notion by veering away toward the south at a sharp angle.

The puff of pale smoke was nearly invisible in the hard sunlight, but he caught the wink of the muzzle flash a couple hundred yards out to his right.

The slug smacked into the dirt to his right front, as usual, and whined nastily away into the desert.

Raider grinned and gave the rifleman a cheerful wave.

"Just checkin'," he shouted.

Not that he felt particularly cheerful or friendly. No point, though, in letting the other guy know that.

He headed east again.

CHAPTER THIRTEEN

Movement.

A pale shape flickered in front of Raider not fifteen yards distant, and the Remington came into his hand without thought.

His heartbeat pounded in his ears and his senses were keenly tuned as he reacted to the unexpected motion from behind a tiny clump of prickly pear.

For just a moment he thought . . .

There was no gunshot, though. No rifle barrel was there. No human form showed itself.

Instead a coyote skulked out of the shadows into sunlight and made a dash for safety.

Raider thumbed the hammer of the heavy Remington and took careful aim.

His slug took the desert dog in the back of its scrawny neck and spilled it end over end in a pile of mangy fur.

Raider let out a yelp of pleasure and broke into a run.

He holstered the revolver and dropped to his knees beside the dead coyote.

It was a scruffy, unpleasant little creature like all its kind, its coat thin and patchy in this hot environment. It was smaller than the coyotes Raider was used to seeing. This one probably weighed no more than fifteen, eighteen pounds. A full-grown yodel dog raised in hospitable country will go twenty-odd pounds or sometimes more.

Raider would have liked to blunder onto a larger one here. But he damn sure wasn't complaining.

He held the carcass upright by the ears and used his knife to slit the critter's throat.

Carefully he smoothed the hair back away from the cut in the still warm flesh, then bent and placed his mouth over the neat incision.

He lifted the carcass overhead now and drank the warm, salty blood, scarcely pausing for breath in his eagerness to take in all the moisture he could.

The blood soothed the dryness in his throat and filled his belly.

It was warm and tasted like shit. And he couldn't get enough of it to suit him.

He drank until the flow stopped and then sucked at the animal's arteries for more, only stopping when the last available drop had been drained from the little coyote.

Only when he was positive there was no more to be had was he willing to let the carcass down. He wiped his bloody chin and mouth and waved off toward the emptiness to the south, telling the rifleman out there that, all right damn it, he felt better now. He was better able to cope and to go on now. Fuck you now.

On an impulse, Raider picked up his knife again and quickly skinned the coyote. Without the patchy gray and piss-yellow fur the carcass looked like that of a housecat.

Raider collected some dry sage and dead greasewood and built a small fire. He cut both skinny hams off the dead coyote and cooked them briefly, only taking time to sear the meager bits of meat.

He ate just one of them, though.

The other he continued to cook over the quickly dying fire until he was done with his meal. Then, his belly full of blood and meat alike now, he kicked the ashes of the fire apart and scattered the embers. He picked up the remaining coyote ham and held it up for the rifleman to see. Then he bent and ostentatiously laid the cooked meat on a clean patch of exposed rock.

"Enjoy yourself," he hollered.

Damn, but he felt better now.

As quickly as that his strength and vigor were back now that he had something substantial in his stomach.

"I'll walk slow," he shouted, "so's you won't have any trouble catching up again after you eat."

He removed his Stetson, the hot but fresh air feeling good on his scalp now, and resettled it. Then he began pacing purposefully once more toward the Virgin Mountains.

He did not look back to see if the rifleman came to claim the meat Raider had left for him.

CHAPTER FOURTEEN

A little bit of fluid, a little bit of food; it was amazing how much better he felt now. Even so, he intended to take nothing for granted. He continued to stop and retrieve cactus pulp to chew on every chance he had. Raider was beginning to feel like he was grazing his way to the Virgins.

There was still no sign of the rifleman anywhere near, but Raider didn't believe for a minute that the ambusher had dropped off.

This job of herding was too deliberate for it to be some kind of harmless amusement that would be casually abandoned.

And those damned Virgin Mountains were much farther away than he'd thought.

Raider was no pilgrim newly come to big country where the clear air and open spaces make distant objects seem miles closer than they really are, but even he had been fooled this time.

After nearly a full day of walking, the Virgins appeared little closer than when he'd started.

It is positively amazing, he reflected, how much a man gets to depend on the solid, steady speed of a horse between his knees when he's traveling.

For a man on horseback, those ugly little mountains would be no more than a nuisance, a minor obstacle to be bypassed.

For a man walking in the desert they seemed an unobtainable goal.

He kept hiking steadily toward them anyway. If the man with the rifle wouldn't let him move south toward the Colorado, Raider would settle for the Virgins. He needed some sort of goal to work toward, and reaching those piles of barren rock seemed a better goal than seeking a bullet in his belly.

Toward dusk he spotted and shot a jackrabbit and drank its blood too, then cooked and ate most of it himself. This time he left only the stringy, tasteless meat of the forelegs and ribs behind for his tormentor with the too-accurate rifle.

Once again, though, he waved cheerfully and pointed to make sure the SOB knew what he was doing.

Damn him, anyway. Bastard.

Raider smiled and pointed and told him to enjoy the meal. Then walked on.

At sundown he stopped.

He gathered brush for a fire even though he had nothing to cook and collected enough extra that he could keep the fire burning into the night.

After last night it was clear that he wasn't going to be able to slip away in the darkness, so he might as well use it to some advantage. Get himself some needed sleep and make that sonuvabitch out there think that Raider wasn't bothered a lick by all this stupidity.

If Raider could force some hint of uncertainty in the

rifleman's thoughts, it would be worthwhile. Anything to put the fellow off balance, by however little. Anything to make the bastard think Raider was unconcerned and cheerful.

He found a shallow depression in the desert floor where he would be protected from the wind at least a little and set up his camp there. Although in this case "camp" consisted only of the fire and a pair of hollows gouged in the ground where his shoulders and hips could lie comfortably.

He took stock of what he had while he was about it.

He'd fired two cartridges today and regretted neither one of them in exchange for the blood and the meat they had delivered.

But his spare ammunition had been in the saddlebags that the rifleman had taken from the corral wall.

Raider removed his gunbelt and examined the bullet loops sewn onto it.

The Remington held five stubby, brass cartridges with one chamber left open for the hammer to rest safely on.

The gunbelt had fifty loops, but now only—he counted—thirty-two cartridges in it.

He cussed himself a little for not keeping the loops full. But then a man didn't think about that sort of thing until he'd already gone and made the mistake. Gunbelt loops were supposed to be a convenience, not a necessity, damn it. A man only thought to refill them when they were running low or he took the notion. Nobody went around worrying about that sort of thing as a general rule of matters.

He had his knife and—again he counted—twenty-three matches.

Pocket watch with winding key. Handkerchief. Wallet with Pinkerton ID and cash. Loose pocket change. Saddle strings. The cash sure as hell wasn't of much account right here and now. Here the paper money was only valuable as tinder, and the coins weren't even good for that.

Not all that much to work with, he conceded.

Enough to work with, he firmly decided.

Fuck this guy, whatever he was up to.

He replaced everything in his pockets but the saddle strings he had collected back at the Blue Walls. Those could be put to use now.

There were no beaten paths to show where small game ran, so Raider operated on the guess-and-by-God principle for deciding where to place his snares.

The dry, desert brush was too flimsy and brittle to try and fashion a snatch snare with live wood bent to act like a spring of sorts. A plain and simple loop noose held open low to the ground and anchored to something reasonably solid would have to do.

If some rabbit or kangaroo rat wanted to commit suicide and strangle itself, Raider would be willing to benefit from its death.

He had four of the leather thongs, so he made four snares and set them where he hoped they might do some good. Or not. He wouldn't know until morning if he had guessed well or poorly.

Once that was done, he had nothing better to do than stare at the stars or else go to sleep.

He'd seen a star before, so he decided on sleep as the better course.

One thing for sure, he thought as he pulled the black Stetson over his face and tugged the collar of his coat higher.

Tonight he wasn't having to worry about being bloated or overfull from too much supper.

He let his breathing slow and tried not to think about the rifleman who was out there somewhere close by in the night.

CHAPTER FIFTEEN

Raider didn't even bother to cuss about finding his snares empty and undisturbed. He hadn't honestly expected to catch anything in them anyway.

He collected them, rolled the thongs up, and stuffed them back into his pocket to be set again later.

The rising sun was hidden behind the Virgins, but its light was strong. The morning was cool and the desert floor lightly shadowed. It would remain that way until the sun cleared the tops of the Virgins.

Raider shoved the toe of his boot through the ashes of last night's fire to make sure there were no embers still alive—pure habit, since there was nothing much here to burn even if he tried to start a prairie fire—and tugged the brim of his hat lower.

That was all the preparation he needed to start the day's journey. That and maybe to take his belt up a notch.

He still felt pretty good, though, after the coyote and the rabbit yesterday. They'd done wonders for him.

And after a good night's sleep, even his feet weren't hurting all that much.

He took a long, close look around the full sweep of the horizon, but there was nothing of particular interest out there.

Certainly there was no sign of the rifleman, damn it.

The only movement he saw was a pair of buzzards riding the morning air currents high overhead.

As he watched, the dark, ugly birds swept lower.

"Yeah, an' a lovely mornin' to you too, you sons o' bitches," he muttered. "But not today. Not me for breakfast."

The big birds were close enough that he thought he might be able to pot one.

Buzzards have blood too. Of course they do.

No reason why a man shouldn't get moisture from buzzard blood, is there?

He made a face.

Maybe no valid reason, then, but reason enough, at least for the moment.

If it hadn't been for the coyote and the rabbit yesterday he might have shot one of the putrid things and taken its blood.

But today he wasn't feeling that desperate. Not yet, he wasn't.

He ignored the creatures and started out at a slow, steady pace toward the east.

There was still no sign of the rifleman.

Raider trusted the bastard to be there.

A thought struck him, and he smiled tightly to himself.

He wanted a look at this asshole, and why not.

Without warning he broke into a hard, leg-stretching, arm-pumping run toward the distant Virgins.

The guy was able to sneak at a walking pace. But how about if he had to try and keep up at a run. Even a coyote can't stay hidden at full speed.

Raider sprinted for nearly three hundred yards, then skidded to a stop and watched the empty country to the south.

"Hah!" he shouted. "There you are!"

A glimpse was all he got. A brief glimpse of a human shape darting to cover behind a low patch of greasewood. But he did get that glimpse.

It was crazy, the sense of triumph that fleeting look gave him.

For a moment he was so wrapped up in enjoying the success that it didn't occur to him to think about the figure he'd just seen.

Then he called it back, remembering it and searching for details that his conscious mind had recorded but not registered at any surface level.

He frowned.

The figure he'd seen was that of a naked body. Or nearly so. Dark and sun-bronzed.

Or an Indian?

Why the fuck would an Indian be wanting to play games with him?

And what Indian?

Apache? There wasn't an Apache reservation for a hundred fifty miles, he was pretty sure, and the nearest remaining bands of hostile Apache were way the hell and gone down in the Sierra Madres of Mexico. And damned few of them left even down there at this point.

Besides, the brief impression he'd gotten hadn't been that of an Apache style of dress to begin with.

If not Apache, what then?

Yaqui? Papago? Yuma? Pah-Ute? Pima?

None of those would make any more sense than an Apache dogging him out here in the middle of nothing.

A half-naked white man, then. A desert hermit, like. Some out-of-his-mind hermit too timid to commit murder, maybe even a religious fanatic who couldn't murder someone but who was willing to try to force an innocent traveler into dying of thirst so the idiot could rob his body afterward?

Raider couldn't honestly say that any of those possibilities made the least bit of sense.

But then the mere fact that he was here made no sense to begin with.

He was almost sure that what he'd seen was a near-naked human figure darting behind that brush, though.

Weird.

He sighed and shook his head, then forced a grin and waved cheerfully toward the low stand of greasewood.

He started walking again. He'd accomplished what he'd wanted to do, by damn, and that was good enough for the moment. He certainly didn't want to abuse the strength he'd regained at this point. Those few hundred yards of running had left him puffing and just a wee bit shaky in the knees. Maybe he hadn't come back quite as far as he'd believed.

He stopped, broke open a cactus no bigger than a pigeon's egg and began chewing the pulp, then moved on again, this time at a slow and steady pace toward the east.

Raider had walked another fifty yards or so before it occurred to him.

That figure back there hadn't been carrying a rifle.

His hands had been empty.

Raider was positive about that.

Positive.

He stopped, brought the impressions back through his mind yet once more and knew good and well that he had truly seen what he had seen.

That half-naked son of a bitch was definitely not carrying a rifle.

"Hah!" Raider shouted toward the silent, motionless greasewood clump. "Gotcha."

He squared his shoulders, made a rude gesture in the direction where he had seen the man, and set off once more.

This time toward the south and the Colorado River.

CHAPTER SIXTEEN

"Oh, shit!"

He jumped as dirt and gravel sprayed practically underneath his left boot. Close this time. That hadn't happened before.

And the gunshot this time had come from *behind* him. Damn.

But he'd seen that shadower to the *front*.

The unarmed shadower, that is. The one he'd been so certain sure had no rifle now. The one he'd *seen* had no rifle in hand.

The one with the rifle, damn him, the *other* one, was to the north now.

So there were two of them. And if there were two where Raider had only expected one, just how many *more* of the sons of bitches might there be?

But...*all* of them so damned good that they could move about undetected and do it pretty much as they pleased?

Obviously, Raider reluctantly conceded.

He didn't like that worth a shit, but there it was, like it or not.

At least they'd gone and answered one question for him. This wasn't some pack of religious hermits communing with God and Nature in the Big Lonesome.

This was some band of Indians, tribe unknown, motives for *sure* unknown.

Raider stood there in plain sight, shrugged again, and made a gesture of "just tryin', pal" toward the seemingly empty desert flats.

The Indian didn't shoot again.

And Raider didn't move south any further either.

Apparently that was all that was desired at the moment.

Fine. Great. Fuck you very much.

Raider made a smart turn to the the left and once more started walking toward the Virgin Mountains.

He couldn't help but wonder just how many folks were wandering through the desert at the moment, everybody seemingly content to follow along and aggravate a certain Pinkerton operative.

Now, of course, he could look for his little band of followers on both sides. To the front and the rear too for all he knew at this point.

But it hardly seemed worth the effort any longer.

Whoever these sons of bitches were, they were almighty good.

Why hadn't they killed him?

Not that he was complaining, mind, but the question nagged and gnawed at him.

They could have. Last night. The night before. Virtually anytime since he hit the Blue Walls. Even before that? He couldn't be sure, of course, but he had to suspect that they'd picked him up there at the Blue Walls. Until then he had been on horseback and moving fast and steady. These Indians were afoot. If they'd had horses he would have seen them. A man can maybe hide on ground this empty, but never a horse.

All right, then, they spotted him at the Blue Walls and started in on this crazy campaign to... to what? That was the question, wasn't it? To fucking *what*?

He hadn't a clue as to why they were doing any of this. He only knew for sure that they were doing it.

Starting at the Blue Walls.

Did that have some significance?

It was too soon to tell for sure.

Raider had been going—had been directed—to the Blue Walls to capture a man who had never showed up.

The Indians either were already there or showed up soon after he did.

On purpose?

He wished to hell he knew.

It was damned unlikely they had been waiting there for the next passing white to show up so they could torment the poor SOB, like for religious reasons. Testing manhood or any of that bullshit. Not that it wasn't something an Indian could or would do; it was just that if they'd wanted something of that nature they would've wanted to capture him for the tormenting, not just drive him around and around in the lousy desert.

Besides, that notion wouldn't stand up simply because there *were* no white travelers at the Blue Walls these days. Sign left at the old station showed that clear enough. A band of Indians wanting to waylay the next available white would be stupid to pick the Blue Walls as their ambush site. And this crowd didn't strike Raider as being particularly stupid.

All right, then, say they just happened by on their way from Here to Over There and lucked into him as a victim of their play.

Possible? Sure. Anything was possible.

Likely? Huh-uh.

Raider was too old a hand at dealing with craziness and skullduggery to put much faith in the likelihoods of coincidence. He just pure and simple didn't believe in coincidence.

So just for the moment, just for the purposes of trying to think this through, he decided, put aside coincidence as the causative factor here and reject as well the idea that the Indians had been waiting at the Blue Walls for any stray travelin' man.

There wasn't a whole helluva lot left to choose from, he realized.

If those Indians hadn't been waiting there for just anybody to show up at the white man's abandoned structure, and if they hadn't just happened to be in the neighborhood when he came along, well, the most glaring other possibility that came to mind was that those unknown Indians had been there waiting for a certain, a very particular that is, Pinkerton man to make an appearance at the never-used Blue Walls.

He frowned.

That made just as little sense as anything else in this nutsy situation.

There wasn't an Indian tribe on the continent that had any particular hard-on for Raider. Not that he knew about.

And Jonas Dial? Dial surely hated each and every Pinkerton operative, but as a collective and general sort of thing. Dial would have no special grudge against Raider. Not more than any other Pinkerton.

This business here smacked strong of grudge. It all seemed so damned deliberate.

Raider had already considered the possibility that he'd been sent on a wild goose chase to the Blue Walls so as to get him out of Chloride and therefore out of Dial's way. That was still entirely possible.

But this? This was more than a simple desire to get somebody chasing into a blind alley just for the purpose of keeping him out of Chloride, Arizona Territory.

Sending him out to the Blue Walls, sure. Even having

his horses killed once he got there, to make certain he wouldn't be able to turn around and rush back again in time to disrupt Mr. Dial's future plans, that might make some sort of sense too.

But why this fol-de-rol with the shadowing and the herding and the constant surveillance?

And why Indians, anyway?

If it was Dial behind it and he just wanted Raider kept clear of Chloride, surely ordering the tipster to provide the bait and send him out to the Blue Walls, where the hook could be set, would have been enough. Then a quick run at the corral by some of his own gang members would have done the rest. They could've attacked Raider and tried to shoot him down at the Blue Walls—that for sure would keep a fella out of the way—or they could have come in in the night and shot or stolen the horses. That would have done the job too.

So what was this horseshit with Indians and shots fired deliberately wide so he would be guided but never harmed? Jonas Dial might want to kill him—but want to carefully keep him alive and go to great lengths to insure it? No chance.

Raider wished like hell he could simply walk over to the nearest warrior of the Whatchamacallit tribe and *ask* the SOB what the big idea was.

He even considered trying it. Just walk over and talk to them. Why not?

He considered it, all right. But briefly. Only briefly.

It wasn't such a bad notion on the surface of things, but every time he gave it some thought there was a feeling somewhere deep in his gut that made him think it wasn't such a good idea after all.

Nothing he could point a finger at or pin down with a sound, logical, reasoned rejection.

It was just a . . . feeling, mixed in with half-conscious impressions about pride and manhood and self-sufficiency and he didn't know what else.

What he did know for sure was that every time he considered the idea of trying to establish contact with those Indians out there, his gut instinct told him to forget it.

That was plenty good enough to go on, he finally concluded.

A learned and respected professor of something-or-other had told him once that human beings don't have instincts, only animals do. Which as far as Raider was concerned only proved that learned and respected folks don't always know as much as they think they do. Call it instinct or precognition or just call it the willies, experience had proved good enough for him that when his gut response to something was this powerful he'd damn sure better snap to and pay attention to what it was telling him.

Better for the time being to let things unravel the way they wanted. When the time came, if the time came, he could do something different then. For right now he would let things slide.

He stopped, spat out the chew of cactus pulp he'd been sucking on, and replaced it with a fresh piece.

Then he marched on toward the Virgins.

CHAPTER SEVENTEEN

He reached the base of the Virgins just before dusk. The timing couldn't have been much better. What he most wanted to see here was most likely to occur at either dawn or dusk.

Up close, he saw, the Virgin Mountains weren't a lick prettier than they'd been from afar.

They were dry, arid, lumpy, and ugly.

If anything, they supported even less vegetation than the desert floor Raider had been crossing all the way from the Blue Walls.

But there was hope. Any damn place at all could offer hope. Ugly and empty as this country seemed, he was hopeful now that he'd gotten here.

He climbed partway up the first rugged hillside he came to, not bothering to try to select likely places in a country he knew nothing about. Nature often is no more logical than people are. And that means not at all.

The footing on the loose slope was terrible. He had to scramble on all fours part of the way, and even then he slid back nearly as much as he moved upward.

He moved up just far enough to get a good look out across the country to the west—and, much more important, the flat country lying along the western fringe of the puny little so-called mountains—and settled down there with his forearms resting on his knees and his hat brim pulled low against the fading remnants of sunlight, setting now somewhere in the direction of California.

It was interesting to see that the Indians knew he'd spotted at least one of them earlier, knew as well that he would be able to spot them easily again from here, and now were giving up their secrecy.

Now that Raider had taken root on an elevated promontory, the band of Indians allowed themselves to move into the open.

There were *eleven* of them. And all he'd seen of them until this moment was a brief and flickering glimpse of *one*.

Damn, but they were good.

Raider took his hat off and saluted them with it.

There wasn't any reaction from down below, but he was sure they saw. He hoped they understood as well.

There really wasn't time right now to concentrate on the Indians, but he couldn't help but spend a moment looking them over.

They stayed too far away—damn careful to stay well outside the range of a pistol shot—for him to get a really good look at them, but what he could see gave him some distinct impressions.

They were a piss-poor bunch. He could tell that clear enough.

There wasn't enough cloth or clothing among them to clothe one city-dressed white woman, not if you assembled it all together. Loincloths seemed to be about the only type of garment any of them possessed, and the kids weren't even wearing that much.

Of the eleven Indians he could see—and there weren't

any actual guarantees that this was all of them—four looked to be men, five women, and two naked children. Come along, kiddies, Mommy and Daddy are gonna go drive a white guy round the bend today. He frowned. Shit, he hadn't even spotted this outfit's children out there in the desert.

Raider consoled himself with the idea that the women and kids probably had been kept well away from the chase.

The thing that really and truly graveled him, though, wasn't that there were women and children in the bunch that was toying with him. It was that in the whole damn crowd there was only one lone firearm.

Just one single rifle was visible to him now.

Raider's *own* damn rifle. That had to be his Winchester that the tall man with the skinny legs was carrying.

If Raider had had sense enough to keep the Winchester in his hands where the thing properly belonged...

He sighed. What-if was not a fun game to play at the best of times and would be an even less attractive pursuit right now. The point was, he hadn't kept the Winchester in his own hands, and now that Indian down there did have it in his, and there wasn't any changing the facts by wistful wishfulness.

It occurred to him that if they hadn't got hold of the rifle they might have acted differently about the way they herded him over here.

Like maybe they wouldn't have felt safe about trying to force his actions and might've been quick to kill him instead.

He didn't for a minute believe that they wouldn't have been capable of it, firearms or no. They had proven that point plenty well back at the Blue Walls when they were able to kill the horses and steal from Raider without his even knowing they were around.

So while they weren't long on firepower, they weren't exactly toothless either. They had knives, bows, and probably throwing sticks. Any of those, or just a big enough rock, will do to kill a man if you can reach him. These boys could reach anyone or anything they pleased.

Raider waved to them and put his attention where it properly belonged right now.

And that was a damn sight closer than those Indians standing out there watching him from the desert floor.

He leaned forward and focused his attention on the jagged seam of ground where flat desert met rugged mountainside.

That right there was what he needed to watch while the sun was setting, and as long as those Indians weren't outright mounting an attack, he could think about them later.

He blinked and shaded his eyes and tried to adjust his thoughts and his attention to thinking about things in terms of moving objects the size of houseflies.

CHAPTER EIGHTEEN

He almost missed seeing it, mostly because he hadn't honestly expected to see anything.

It was exactly what he needed, though, if not what he'd expected.

The honeybee flew in off the desert floor just before sundown and droned in its straight, wonderful, delightfully helpful beeline up and to Raider's left.

He chuckled and turned to stare, following the tiny thing until it was out of sight, its small body lost to view against the dull background of rock and sun-dried dirt.

Raider really had been expecting to spot a mourning dove, and that only if he got lucky, but the bee was even better.

Until sixty, seventy years ago, or so he was told, there hadn't been any bees this side of Missouri or maybe Arkansas, with their thickly forested Ozarks. It had been the westward shove of white settlement, the farms really, that spread honeybees where there didn't used to be any.

Now, by damn, they were all the way out here in the middle of nothing.

And bees, bless them, go to water morning and night just like doves do.

Spotting a bee meant that there was water available someplace close.

Raider scrambled across the slope of the hillside until he was directly underneath the path where the bee had just flown.

He crouched there and peered in that direction like he was taking aim down a rifle's sights.

Somewhere in that direct line of sight he would find water.

It might be a mile or more away, but it was there. He could find it. He *would* find it.

He leaned down and quickly built a small cairn of pebbles to mark the starting point he needed to work away from, then glanced up again and made mental note of a landmark on the mountainside above.

Only then did he look away from the beeline to see what the Indians were doing.

They could see what his actions had been. Would they realize what those actions meant?

More to the point, was that tall Indian going to use the rifle to see that Raider couldn't reach the water?

"Playtime is over, son," Raider said softly into the twilight. "Now we all know the game. Enough of it. And I figure to get to that water now whether you like it or not."

The Indians were standing grouped together some two hundred yards away in the gathering dark. The light was too poor and the distance too great for him to make out exactly how many were standing where he could see them.

All eleven? He thought perhaps fewer. He suspected the rest of them were deliberately making it difficult for him to keep track of their whereabouts.

Fair enough.

Raider still had no idea why they were doing any of this. It still had no obvious logic to it.

But at least now he knew what he was facing.

Now at least he could start doing something about it.

He could figure out the rest of it later.

He pulled his shirttail out and used his knife to cut a thin strip off it, then wedged that under the cairn marker he had already built. He wanted to be able to find the spot again come daylight.

Just to be sure, though, he made a few mental references as well, calculating that his cairn was on a line between that stone and this one and again on a line between that lump of earth and this yellow-streaked gray rock. Where those two lines intersected was where his marker should be.

And from that point all he had to do was sight up the mountainside to that . . . yeah, he was sure he could find his starting point come morning. Not before, though. Crawling around at night in country this precipitous was the same as asking for a broken leg. He didn't think he wanted one of those right now, thank you.

Once he was satisfied that he could find the beeline to water again, Raider slid down to the level ground below.

He figured he could set his snares overnight, just in case, get a good night's sleep, and be ready to do some climbing come morning.

Why, a man couldn't ask for much more than that, could he?

From ground level the small band of Indians was invisible to him. He stood and waved in the direction where he had last seen them and hollered, "G'night, all. See you in the morning."

Then he set about placing his snares and preparing his dry and meager camp.

CHAPTER NINETEEN

Morning was dry. He needed to find that water today or he would begin losing strength again. Today, though, he had no doubt that he would finally have something better to drink than blood.

He had wakened just once during the night, when he heard the skittering of loose rock some distance away. He'd come awake with the Remington in his hand but a satisfied smile tugging at his lips. The Indians were messing about on the mountainside. But not too near. Definitely not anywhere near. That was all right. Surely they already knew about the water source Raider intended to find. If they expected to keep him from it, surely they would have tried to take him during the night.

He shrugged. Or maybe not. He still couldn't figure out what this crazy bunch was up to.

Standing upright and shivering twice was all the preparations he needed to make for the start of the new day. It seemed an efficient enough way to get the day going, much less time-consuming than washing up and shaving and all that crap. Although he had to admit that he was beginning to get itchy under the jawline where his whiskers weren't yet quite long enough to soften and his collar occasionally aggravated them.

There wasn't any sign of the Indian tribe now, and no smoke or dust to show where they might have spent the night. Somewhere up ahead in the Virgins waiting for him to catch up to them, he would have guessed. And at least a few of them watching him just to make sure he did what was expected. Fair enough.

He checked his snares, collecting the thongs and replacing them in his pocket as he went, and found a young jackrabbit in the third trap he'd set. He killed the thing quickly and drank its blood, then took the time to light a fire and cook it before he set out onto the mountain.

As before he left the roasted rib cage and a front quarter for the Indians.

Then he climbed back up to the spot where he'd left his cairn.

Again a tight smile thinned his lips. These boys weren't big on making things easy for a fella.

The cairn was there, all right, and the cloth marker easily visible to point it out.

Except neither cairn nor marker was where he'd put them.

They'd been moved a good thirty feet from the place where his mental reference points told him they should be.

Playful sons of bitches, these desert Indians.

Raider cheerfully carried everything back where it ought to be and emplaced them exactly as before.

If the Indians wanted to play, damn it, he'd show them that they weren't winning that easy.

He took the time to put everything just as it had been, then made his line-of-sight calculations and began climbing.

He reached the summit of the first ridge within twenty minutes and stopped there.

It's one thing to follow an imaginary line when there are two or more reference points in sight. But it's an impossibility to follow that line when only one point can be seen, no matter how good a man *thinks* he is in rough country.

Once Raider dropped below the ridgetop he would no longer be able to see the cairn and marker, so he took pains to choose more route markers along his line of march. A wisp of sage here, a lump of ochre rock there, a runty and struggling juniper no taller than a man's boot.

Only when he had his route markers firmly in mind did he give any attention to the country that lay ahead and below.

Then again he smiled.

Halfway up the next hillside and on a direct line with his route markers he could see a dark shadow marking a narrow rock ledge. Sunlight wouldn't reach beneath the ledge for hours if at all.

While Raider watched, a bird flew down the small, canyon-like wrinkle between this ridge and the next one. It lifted toward the shadowed ledge and fluttered out of sight beneath it. It or another like it flew out again moments later. Another departed. Two more arrived.

Underneath that ledge was an improbable place for a nest. Too accessible to cats and other predators. So it was water the birds were finding there, the same water the bees used.

Even so, he stood where he was and searched the countryside carefully for any sign of the Indians. He had no expectation that they had grown tired of their game and gone away. They would be somewhere near. Wherever they were, though, they were staying carefully out of sight. He was willing for them to stay that way for quite as long as they wished.

"Make up your minds," he said loudly. "I'm going over now."

There was no answer except a soughing of the morning breeze sweeping down over the Virgins.

Raider skittered on his boot heels down into the gorge and began climbing again.

His hands and feet were busy with the loose rock on the slope, but his eyes were in constant movement searching the ridges above.

If they wanted to keep him from the water...

There was no gunshot. No ambush.

He reached the depression beneath the ledge and paused there to look around before he bellied down and slid underneath the jagged rock.

He could smell the water before he could see it. Could feel the moisture of it fresh and clean on his skin before he ever touched it.

The tiny, shaded seep was a natural stone basin hidden deep in the rock, a small exposure of the underground aquifer that collected the rare rain and snowfall in this barren country and held it inside the earth.

The opening to it was so narrow that neither man nor horse would ever be able to drink directly from it. Only one or two small birds at a time would be able to drink there. Raider reached inside the opening and felt cool water close over his hand. He smiled.

The exposed basin could hold no more than three or four cups of water, but he hoped that that amount would be nearly constant, whatever was removed being replaced by seepage flowing in to maintain some unknown balance. That was often the way with such hidden seeps.

He cupped his palm and lifted out one handful after another, drinking deeply and wiping his wet hand over his face before reaching in to drink again.

The hat-sized pool did not diminish.

Only when he was sure he would not be emptying the

miniature *tinaja* did he uncap the canteen and begin pouring water into it one palmful at a time.

He filled the canteen and was pleased to see that his makeshift repair leaked only a little, the leather plug quickly swelling and closing off the knife cut in the bottom. Then he filled the container to the brim once more, replacing what little had been lost, and drank cupped handfuls of water again and again.

The water was sweet and invigorating. He filled his belly with it and forced himself to drink more, saturating his tissues with all the fluid he could hold and then some. A stomachache was of no consequence now.

The pool of water was lower now, he realized, but only by a little. He had taken out more than a gallon of life-giving water, but the hidden pond still held at least two cups of water and seemed to be recovering already. He held a fingertip against the bottom of the seep and felt the water level slowly rise toward his knuckle. The water loss was already being replaced. Raider was glad. The Indians would be needing this water too, and the birds and desert insects and whatever else depended on it for their survival. He would have taken the water for himself anyway. That was a matter of *his* survival. But he was glad he didn't have to leave with the knowledge that he had taken it all and left nothing behind.

He wiped his chin and scuttled backward on his belly to withdraw from the ledge.

When he turned and pushed himself into a sitting position on the hillside he was peering into three dark, leathery faces.

And one Winchester muzzle.

CHAPTER TWENTY

"My compliments," Raider said easily. "I wouldn't of thought anybody could get this close to me and be so quiet about it. Especially not on this gravel." He waggled a finger to indicate the loose scree he meant.

If any of the Indians understood English, they were good about hiding the fact. Their solemn expressions never changed. The barrel of the pointing Winchester did not waver.

Raider felt relaxed and confident now. At this range the Remington in his holster was more than the equal of the Winchester. And the Indian who was holding on to the rifle obviously had no idea just how quick a man can get a handgun into action. The rifle wasn't even cocked. Probably the poor fella thought he had Raider covered. Raider honestly hoped that he wouldn't have to give these boys a demonstration of who was in the real danger here.

"Thirsty?" Raider stood, the cartilage in his knee joints popping, and moved aside from the opening to the seep. He motioned for the Indians to go ahead if they wished. No language was needed for that.

The Indians exchanged glances, and the two who had no firearms came forward to drop down and reach into the *tinaja* for a single handful of water each. They lifted the liquid to their lips and drank of it sparingly.

They weren't really thirsty, Raider saw. They were accepting his invitation as a matter of etiquette, not need. Interesting. The one with the rifle blinked and shuffled half a step down the hillside. His foot moving on the loose gravel made as much noise as anybody's now that he wasn't trying to be sneaky quiet.

Raider smiled and hunkered down beside the two who had just gotten drinks. "What d'we do now, boys?" he asked.

One of the Indians said something in a language Raider was fairly sure he'd never heard before. It was so much grunting and mumbling as far as he could make out, which was probably what they heard when he spoke English to them.

Up close and in broad daylight he still had no idea what tribe they might be from.

Not Apache or Navajo, he was sure. Nor any Yumas either, he didn't think. All of those went in for the wearing of clothes nowadays, and if these boys had ever owned a shirt they must've found better things to do with the cloth than to wear it.

Clothing to this crowd seemed to consist of a bit of rag—the one with the rifle in his hands didn't even go for that much modern foofaraw; he stuck to soft leather instead of cloth—no bigger than would wipe a man's ass, tucked under the crotch and held front and rear by a waist thong. It was a practice that sure would minimize a man's wardrobe requirements, Raider decided.

There wasn't a shoe or sandal among them. They were all completely barefoot despite the conditions they traveled in, but the bottoms of their feet looked to be as hard as baked brick, the skin thickened with callus so that they looked as dry and cracked as a desert lake bed.

Their hair was greased and tied in short clubs at the backs of their necks. Two of them wore shell necklaces suspended from leather thongs. The one with the rifle had a lump of quartz for a necklace instead of a seashell. The pale quartz had a shape that might have been a bird fetish. Or maybe not. Raider couldn't help but wonder where in hell the other two would have found seashells out here.

Each of the three carried a knife suspended in a leather pouch hung from their waist thongs, and the two without firearms carried weak, crude bows and a handful of arrows each. They were so primitive that they seemed not to have figured out quivers yet for the convenient carrying of their arrows. That primitive, Raider amended, or maybe just that poor.

Their bows, he noticed, weren't the handsome and shapely things that could still be found among the diehard traditionalists of the plains tribes. These weapons were three, four-foot-long sticks with a leather string tied into notches at either end.

The arrows were smaller sticks, and not particularly straight ones at that, with flaked stone tips and drab bird feather fletching tied instead of glued in place.

All in all pretty damned crude tools for survival in a most demanding country.

"Look, boys, this whole thing has been a lotta fun, I'm sure, but I got things to do now." He smiled and settled back into a sitting position with his arms wrapped around his knees. He tipped his Stetson back and added, "So you tell me. How d'we back off and leave each other be now that we've come this far with it?"

The one with the rifle grunted and looked up the hillside toward the ridge top some fifty feet higher.

He motioned, and a moment later Raider could hear the sound of gravel being dislodged. The fourth warrior, Raider assumed without looking around to see. He already knew that from that distance one of these puny bows would be little threat to him. The one he wanted to keep an eye on was the guy with the Winchester in his hands.

Raider continued to smile, and just for the hell of it he gave the other two a wink.

CHAPTER TWENTY-ONE

Raider blinked with surprise and came to his feet.

It wasn't the fourth warrior who'd come down the mountainside but a girl. A young woman, really. He had no trouble figuring that out because she was dressed almost exactly like the warriors were. Skimpy loincloth. In her case a headband instead of her hair being clubbed. Shell necklace. And she had added a bracelet to the ensemble. It was three different shades of leather braided together and tied around her wrist.

He couldn't claim that she was actually pretty. Her face was too broad and her features too heavy for that. But she had proud, perky, young-looking breasts that would have been much more attractive if they hadn't been quite so filthy. It occurred to him that all of these Indians looked like they'd never heard about bathing. And for that matter, maybe they hadn't.

The man with the rifle—Raider judged that one to be in his thirties or so; all the rest were considerably younger—said something to the girl, and she turned and gave Raider a shy look like she thought he might bite.

The chief, or headman or whatever he might like to be called, said something else. He sounded like he was insisting on something. The girl dropped her eyes and said something back to him. Raider wished to hell he could understand what they were talking about.

He looked away from the chief long enough to glance up the hill in the direction the girl had just come from. All the rest of the band was up there staring down at him now—the fourth warrior, the other women, and the two kids, who he could see now were a boy of eight or so and a girl of maybe ten. He could see now too that one of the women was carrying an infant in her arms. He hadn't spotted the baby in the gloom last evening.

Was it possible that a primitive, desert tribe of Indians would bring the whole band along, women and children included, to watch the capture and torture of a stranger in their land?

Hell yes, he decided.

But he hoped that wasn't what they had in mind. Not that he was the one in any danger now, but none of them was likely to know that.

He yawned and waited for the chief and the young woman to decide what they were doing.

One of the other men nearby gave a yip that left Raider reaching for the Remington, then bolted in the other direction at a run with the other man close behind him.

Raider could see then what they were doing. A jackrabbit's ears had appeared beside a rock. The rabbit probably was coming to water. Now the two Indians seemed intent on chasing the thing down. Afoot. And barefoot at that.

They were also, he noticed, doing a helluva good job of it.

The two men yipped and shouted and plunged across the rocky mountainside without seeming to pay the least bit of attention to where they were running.

Neither of them bothered with their bows. Without breaking stride or slowing down in the slightest, each of them snatched up a fist-sized rock.

They closed the distance on the jackrabbit, and the man nearer the jack threw his rock. He missed but made the rabbit jink into a new direction, and the second man was able to get closer to it for his throw. The rock caught the jackrabbit on the back of the head and spilled it unconscious onto the gravel. The first man grabbed it before it could regain its senses. He held it aloft and shouted something and got back a shout of approval from the audience on top of the ridge. Raider hoped the lone jackrabbit wasn't what the whole band figured to share for supper.

The two hunters were grinning as they came loping back up the hillside with a now dead rabbit in hand.

Raider turned back to the chief and the girl, who seemed to have worked out whatever they'd been talking over.

The girl moved a hesitant step or two closer to Raider. She frowned in deep concentration and said, "You . . . live. Not afraid."

"I'm not afraid," Raider agreed. "And I figure to keep on living, yes."

She nodded and turned to say something to the headman.

She had some English, obviously, but he guessed not much. He hoped it would come back to her with use, because there was a hell of a lot he wanted to ask these folks.

"You not run. Not die," she said.

"Was I supposed to?"

She had to think about that for a bit, probably trying to sort out the words. Then she nodded.

"Quaint customs, you people have," he said.

That quite plainly went over her head. Not that it

mattered. He smiled. "I can't say I'm sorry that I let you down about that."

She might have gotten at least some of that. She thought it over for a moment, then smiled too, turned, and said something to the headman.

The headman's expression didn't change much, but his belly quivered and rolled a little, and Raider thought the guy might be laughing.

The headman—this little band wasn't big enough that Raider could seriously think of him as the chief of anything—said something to the girl and pointed up the hill.

"Come," she told Raider. "You come now. Safe. No more . . ." She ran out of English for that one, tried to think of something that would convey the thought, and gave it up with a shrug. "Come," she repeated.

Raider glanced toward the sun and considered refusing. After all, there was plenty of daylight left, and the Colorado River was still a long way off.

But damn it he wanted to get some answers from these people before he left.

And there was no worry about water for the time being. He had the full canteen and knew where to get more when he wanted it.

He could spare a little time now to see if he couldn't find out the what and the why of this business.

"Sure," he said pleasantly. "After you." He motioned for the girl and the headman to lead the way, and was pleased to see that the man with the rifle didn't hesitate about showing his back to Raider as the three of them climbed the ridge to join the rest of the band there.

CHAPTER TWENTY-TWO

The Indians seemed more excited about the rabbit the hunters had killed than they did about the presence of a white man among them. Raider began to think maybe he'd done more than he suspected when he went and left those few scraps of meat behind. He'd only intended that as a way of thumbing his nose at them, but maybe they had taken it as considerably more.

It appeared that mealtime occurred whenever and wherever there was a meal to be had.

The band jumped into action without hardly a glance at Raider. The women piled up twigs and lumps of dried dung for a fire, and the headman brought out a cracked and filthy but still operable magnifying glass that he used to start a fire.

While that was smoldering and beginning to blaze, the women were busy preparing a stew of rabbit and roots and some unidentifiable bits of something that might have been songbird carcasses. They pitched it all together in a tin pot taken out of a bundle carried by the oldest of the women and poured water in from a greasy skin bag. Dinner, Raider figured. He hoped he wasn't going to have to eat any of the shit. Guts, head, bones and all went into the mess. Obviously these people didn't go in for any niceties. They wanted to get every scrap of nourishment possible out of whatever they found to eat.

The headman peered proudly at the stew mixture, then motioned Raider to a seat on the ground next to him. Raider sat, and the other men drew close around so that a circle was formed.

The headman said something over his shoulder, and the oldest woman—she would be his wife, Raider guessed—brought him a leather pouch that she handled with reverent care.

He rummaged inside the thing and withdrew an age-worn pipe of the red soapstone that Raider knew was quarried a thousand miles or more away from this lonesome spot in the Virgin Mountains. The pipe had a reed stem and a bowl that had been rubbed smooth by what might have been generations of hands.

The headman solemnly filled the thing with a dried weed that Raider didn't recognize, then lighted it not from the cooking fire but with another application of the burning glass.

He took his puffs and exhaled them to earth, sky, and each of the four winds, then handed the pipe to Raider, who did the same before passing it to the next man in the circle.

The substitute tobacco tasted like coyote shit. And indeed it might have been.

The headman said something in a deep, sonorous voice, and Raider nodded his agreement with whatever the hell it was the man was saying.

That seemed to please everybody.

This wasn't any social smoke, he realized quickly. When the pipe got back to the headman it wasn't passed around again. Instead the remaining weed was carefully unloaded onto a flat rock. The headman crushed the coals out with the ball of his thumb—Raider managed to avoid wincing at that, but he wanted to—and both the pipe and the unburned tobacco were returned to the pouch.

Raider was sure the whole procedure had significance, but he hadn't a clue as to what that might be. He settled for smiling and trying to look agreeable.

Once the pouch had been returned to the woman's care, the men turned chatty and laughing, yammering back and forth among themselves and acting like the white man among them was an old and true pal.

And this was the same crowd that'd been stalking him practically from the minute he arrived at the Blue Walls?

None of this made a lick of sense.

The girl who almost spoke English came over and squatted outside the circle, positioning herself behind and between Raider and the headman.

Maybe, Raider thought, he would be able to get some answers now.

He turned to question her but was interrupted by a child's shout.

Over on the other side of the fire, the naked eight-year-old boy was yelping and pointing to a spot high on the next hillside.

The women set up a clamor, and the men all came to their feet in a hurry, grabbing for their weapons.

For a moment Raider thought they were under attack.

Then he spotted what the boy was pointing at.

Close to the peak on the next ridge over, he could see the faintly discernible tan hides of a band of desert bighorn sheep.

The animals' color blended so naturally into the color of the rock that it was difficult to be sure how many of them there were. Three at least, but probably more.

From ridge to ridge the distance was only two hundred yards or so, although it would be a run of at least half a mile to cross the rugged terrain to get there.

The Indian men seemed intent on doing exactly that, going after the skittish sheep afoot and with only their puny bows to hunt with.

Even one sheep, though, Raider realized, would feed the entire band for several days.

The headman, oddly, seemed to give no thought to the Winchester that could so easily reach across that distance and knock down a sheep with ease. Maybe, Raider thought, the guy wasn't such a good rifle shot after all. Hell, for all Raider knew the headman might have been trying to hit him with those wide-ranging bullets he'd fired over the past couple of days.

"Wait!" Raider barked on an impulse.

The headman paused and looked at him, and the girl translated.

Raider stepped forward, pointed to the rifle, and held out his hand palm upward.

The headman hesitated for only a moment. He gave the rifle to Raider with a look like he'd just lost his best friend.

Raider glanced down at the Winchester. It was his own. But then he'd already as good as known that.

He checked the loading gate and saw there was at least one cartridge in the magazine. He worked the lever and empty brass flew. The headman had braced him down there by the seep with an empty chamber. No, this guy didn't know a helluva lot about firearms.

Raider took another moment to look the rifle over and decided that the sights probably hadn't been bumped askew.

Two hundred yards wasn't an exceptionally long shot, but he wanted to be sure.

He sat on the hilltop facing half away from the sheep and took a brace against his upraised knees, then leaned over the sights and aimed with much more care than he normally would use.

A ewe near the top of the far ridge looked fat and healthy. With luck he could drop her and spook the rest of the bunch downhill into the gorge instead of up and over the top where they would be out of sight for a following shot.

With luck he might have time to get three or even four shots off before the sheep skedaddled.

He took a breath, let half of it out, and squeezed off the first round, aiming at a point immediately behind the foreleg of the fat ewe.

The Winchester rocked back against his shoulder, and automatically his hand fanned the lever.

He didn't need to wait to see the results of the first bullet. He knew where that one was going, and that ewe would be dead before she ever fell.

Now was the tricky part.

The rest of the bunch bolted, jumping first uphill in response to the sound, then spinning and running down again as the ewe above them dropped.

Perfect.

There were more of them than he'd seen to begin with. Now that they were in motion it was easy to spot them. There were at least seven sheep left in the flock.

He picked up another ewe, then swung the sights away from it when he saw a lamb running at its heels. Better to save those for next year's meat. He settled instead on a smallish ram, took a lead on the running sheep, and fired again. The ram tumbled end over end down the rocks.

He worked the lever again, picked a target, and squeezed.

The rifle snapped on an empty chamber, damn it. The headman hadn't kept the magazine full.

Raider had no choice now but to set the Winchester aside. There were neither time nor language to ask where the spare cartridges had gotten to.

The sheep scampered into the bottom of the gorge and raced out of sight to the south.

Raider was a bit miffed that he'd only been able to knock down two of the sheep.

The Indians, on the other hand, were practically delirious with the sight of all that meat lying on the rocks over there.

The three grown men and the small boy went shrieking off to retrieve the dead bighorns, and the women shouted and danced until Raider thought they were going into convulsions. He might've said something about it all except his translator was acting just as crazy as the rest of them.

The headman was beaming and babbling and thumping Raider on the shoulders and hippety-hopping around in small circles.

Raider shrugged. It didn't really seem all that big a deal as far as he was concerned.

One nice thing, though. He was willing to think now that these folks weren't much interested in murdering him at this point. Assuming they had been to begin with, that is. He still couldn't quite decide about that. It was probably just as well that it no longer seemed to matter.

He smiled and resigned himself to waiting for the excitement to die down so he could maybe get some answers about all this.

CHAPTER TWENTY-THREE

The Indians' excitement was more serious, and took a hell of a lot longer, than Raider would have believed.

There was chanting and dancing going on literally for hours as the two sheep were butchered and the smaller one, the ram, put on the fire immediately to roast.

The rabbit-and-trash stew wasn't forgotten. It was shared around and gobbled up. But it was the sheep that was the center of interest now.

While the ram cooked, the meat of the ewe was cut into thin strips and laid out to dry. The stewpot was filled again with brains, guts, and marrow from both sheep, and that nauseating mixture was left to simmer.

Even the men were busy fetching burnable materials now. Firewood when they could find it. Inedible roots and dung when they couldn't.

They scoured the mountainsides quite literally for more than a mile around to drag in anything that looked like it would burn.

Hard damn country, Raider saw. He didn't envy anybody who was trying to make a living out here.

As the guest of honor, or so he figured, he didn't seem to be required to participate in any of this, but he decided what the hell. He was willing to earn his keep.

He walked out like the rest of them and fetched in twigs and roots and a hatful of dried sheep shit to add to the fire.

He found it interesting that no one seemed to object when he wandered off on his own. No one shadowed him and nobody reached for any weapons. Acceptance with this bunch apparently ran deep and full.

Raider made sure he was too busy to be bothered when that first pot of stew was passed around—it wouldn't have been polite to refuse if it'd been actually offered—but he was ready enough to participate when it came to putting the roast ram away.

The young ram's meat was delicious. The animal hadn't been old enough for the flavor to turn strong yet, and it was served up however a body liked, do-it-yourself style. Whenever a chunk of the charred, piping-hot meat was wanted, a knife and a grimace and some stinging fingers were what were required. The meat was cut away from the carcass as quickly as the outside was more or less done and the whole roasting thing was still lying on rocks beside the fire.

Even the kids had to help themselves if or when they wanted to eat.

And did they want to eat?

By mid-afternoon there wasn't anything left of the ram but bones. And those had been cracked open and the hot marrow extracted too.

A desert bighorn isn't near the size of the mountain varieties, but even so the dozen people had consumed a helluva lot of fresh meat.

Raider had thought he'd done his share at putting that

ram away until he took a look across the fire at the little girl in the band.

The kid was a skinny little thing of ten or so, not yet old enough to bother with wearing any more clothes than a necklace, certainly not old enough to begin developing like a woman, but she was plenty old enough to pack the groceries away.

She sat there grinning at him, grease practically to her ears and more of it running down her arms to drip off her elbows. She sat there giggling and grinning and wolfed down a good two pounds of half-raw mutton. And that was just at that sitting, in between chores of fetching wood and water. She'd already been at the carcass at least once before that Raider recalled, and she came back again afterward and ate more until her belly was distended so that she almost looked pregnant years before that would be possible.

Raider winked at her and helped himself to a sliver of pinkish meat that had a thin line of crisp, curling fat clinging to it.

The little girl giggled and hid her eyes but acted like she was pleased with the attention.

These Indians were plenty different from anybody Raider had ever run across before. But they were the same in other ways, too.

He looked for the little boy and discovered the kid—who was something of a hero for having spotted the bighorn flock to begin with—hanging around behind him not three feet away.

The boy was eyeing the blued steel of the Winchester like the rifle was something mystical.

Raider motioned him closer—that didn't require much in the way of persuasion, actually—and showed him how a rifle functions.

That part was easy enough without a common language, but it was considerably more difficult trying to explain how the sights were to be used.

He noticed the headman moving in over Raider and the boy and pretending not to be paying attention, so Raider slowed down and started that part over again. This time he drew pictures in the dirt to show the blade of the front sight should be lined up in the notch of the rear leaf and then how the whole thing should be centered on a target. He was pretty sure he eventually got the idea across to the boy. He was less sure how much the headman understood, since he was still pretending that he was looking elsewhere.

"Take," the English-speaking young woman told him when he was done with the lessons. She held out his saddlebags but looked almighty unhappy about it. So did the rest of the band. They were doing the decent thing by him, but they were giving up riches of incalculable value in doing so, he knew. Ordinary enough stuff to Raider, but real riches to them.

Raider thought about it and held in a sigh. He got a fistful of rifle cartridges out of the saddlebags and showed the boy, with the headman watching again, how to load them into the rifle.

Then quick before he could change his damn mind he carried saddlebags and rifle both over to the headman and made a show of presenting them to the fellow as gifts freely given.

Shit, a person would've thought he had gone and made them all crowned princes or something.

The celebration over the two sheep hadn't been half what this one turned out to be.

Raider still wasn't sure if he was more peeved with himself for doing it or pleased for the Indian band's sake.

But he had to admit that he wouldn't have taken it back now even if he could.

Hell, he could buy another Winchester in any store he cared to walk into.

To these folks it was something marvelous.

Made a man think, by damn.

He sat back, his belly full, and enjoyed watching as the Indians celebrated through the rest of the afternoon and on into the night.

CHAPTER TWENTY-FOUR

Raider was tired. The Indians were still celebrating. He finally gave up expecting any answers to his many questions, at least for the time being, and walked off away from the fire in search of a good place to bed down.

It wasn't as if that was going to be a complicated process. He didn't have to worry himself about things like blankets and bedrolls, since everything he'd had with him of that nature was either tucked away in one of the bundles owned by an Indian or was abandoned back there at the Blue Walls.

All he had to do to declare himself abed was to lie down on a soft-looking spot and say it was so.

He kicked hollows in the gravel for his hips and shoulders and flopped. Just to be somewhat formal about the process he pulled his boots off and tipped his hat over his eyes. That took care of the distraction of the firelight—if not the noise of the chanting and the stomping that was still going on around the fire.

He hadn't much more than started to relax well when

he was interrupted by the approach of footsteps. He pushed the hat off his eyes and squinted to see who it was.

It was the girl who thought she spoke English. She smiled at him.

"Hello," he told her.

"H'lo, Ray-der."

He blinked. He was pretty sure he couldn't recall the exchanging of names with anybody here.

Yet this girl knew who he was right down to his name. Without any of them ever asking.

And she *had* admitted that he'd been expected to die in the damn desert.

There were some questions here that he was simply going to have to get the answers to.

But, uh, maybe not right now?

The young woman stood there beside Raider's makeshift bed, in plain view of every other member of the band, with the firelight making coppery highlights on her dusky skin, and got herself undressed.

Not that there was all that much involved in that process, of course.

All she had to do to strip was to untie the thong around her waist the let her loincloth drop away.

Funny how she looked naked now but really hadn't just a moment earlier.

She was still smiling.

Her hands fluttered, sketching outlines of her own body in the air. She cupped her breasts toward him and grinned, then reached down and pressed a hand over her crotch. She was by damn offering herself to him.

Raider looked past her to the headman and the other warriors. They had paused in their dancing and were smiling at him.

Surely one of those fellas over there was the woman's husband. This band wasn't big enough to allow any unmarried, unproductive people in it. A group this size needed all the children they could produce just to stay up with the work of trying to gather food for everybody.

Yet everybody seemed quite agreeable to the idea that this particular member of the bunch should come over and screw their guest.

"Hospitable of y' all," Raider drawled.

All of them were smiling now. Waiting to see if he accepted the offer? Hell, he would probably insult them if he sent the girl packing. Turning down one of their women might be worse to their way of thinking than turning down their food.

But he sure as hell wished they would decide to look someplace else.

The girl knelt beside him and touched his crotch. Her eyes went a little wider after that. She began tugging at his belt buckle.

"Better let me do that," Raider suggested. He stood to get out of his clothes and the natural reaction he was having to her offer was there for all to see. He tried to ignore the whispering that the other women were doing now.

The girl took his hand and pulled him down onto the ground again. She didn't seem to mind in the slightest that it was bare, gravel-sprinkled dirt they were lying on. She snuggled in close to him with a giggle and a grab at his cock.

"Shy, huh?" he asked.

She was direct enough about it. No demands here for kissing and foreplay. She spread herself wide and scooted underneath him, a firm grip around his pecker making sure he came along to where she wanted him, and scissored her legs firm around him.

She wasn't particularly wet, and he wouldn't have thought she was anything close to being ready, but she didn't wait around about it.

She lifted herself to him and pulled Raider down onto

her, and he slid inside the dry heat of her quick as a rabbit.

Most any other woman he'd ever been with would have squealed from the pain of such an abrupt entry, but this girl's smile never wavered. Dry as she was she took all of him and took it all at once.

Raider held himself deliberately still and after a moment felt her tissues moisten around him. Only then did he begin to pump slowly in and out.

He didn't have any trouble at all holding himself back so she could catch up and maybe have some fun out of it too.

Aside from the fact that a neighborly fuck hadn't at all been on his mind lately, so that it was taking him a bit of time to adjust to this new notion, the gravel under his knees hurt like hell.

And then there was the aroma that went along with the experience.

It was truly a good thing, he suspected, that man was designed with his nose kept considerable distance from his pecker, because this woman hadn't had a bath since the last time she fell into a river. He suspected too that ass wiping wasn't much in vogue around here. Although to be fair about it he had to admit that anything locally available for that purpose was likely to have thorns on it.

The smell was bad enough to make him wish for a sudden head cold, and it wasn't helped any by the cat shit, or whatever, that was used as hairdressing material here.

Raider had cleaned out hog wallows that smelled better than this girl's hair did.

He had to give her credit for vigor, though. Now that she was wet and into the spirit of things, she was humping and pumping for all she was worth.

Strap her backside to a springpole rig, he suspected,

and you'd have a well drilled in and producing in no time flat.

She began grunting and keening low in her throat, and damned if he didn't find himself caught up in it too now.

All of a sudden she didn't smell quite so bad. And she sure as hell felt about as good as it gets.

Raider closed his eyes and his mind and let the natural course of things take over.

The Indian girl shuddered and convulsed under him, the lips of her pussy contracting so powerfully it might have hurt, except that it damn sure didn't, and he felt his own surge of release building and building and finally erupting.

He stiffened and plunged forward, pinning her onto the rocks without complaint as he spewed hot fluids from his body into hers.

She hugged him to her with her arms and legs alike, and he was aware now that her breathing was ragged and coming in short gasps.

Not that he could fault her for that. So was his.

He grinned and pulled back a little, although not completely out.

"Wow," he said.

She giggled and looked over his shoulder.

Raider turned his head to see what she was staring at.

The other members of the band, all of them right down to the little kids, had drifted near and now were standing over the two of them.

Raider felt himself commence to shrivel. He dropped free of her body with a loose, moist, plopping sound.

Fortunately, he saw, everybody was still smiling.

Which didn't make him feel the least bit better about the audience.

He let out a long, slow breath and wondered just how silly he would look if he began scrambling for his clothes.

Pretty silly, he decided.

He settled for smiling and nodding. And staying the hell belly down so at least *every*thing wasn't out there on display.

CHAPTER TWENTY-FIVE

"How d'you know my name?" Raider asked. He and the girl were sitting near the quickly dying fire, with the other members of the band gathered close around. He hadn't exactly been sleepy again after finding himself to be a public performer. Now that the dancing was stopped and the gathering was informal, the women were permitted in the circle along with the menfolk. The headman was on Raider's other side.

"You Ray-der, yes?"

He nodded.

"I..." She said something that might have been a Greek word pronounced backwards. She pointed to the headman and gave his name too, then one by one reeled off the names of each of the others except for the little boy. Maybe he didn't have a name yēt. None of the name sounds were anything that Raider's tongue would ever fit around.

"Pleased to meet you," he said. "But what I need to know is how you have *my* name."

She frowned, apparently concentrating on the English sounds. He repeated it, more slowly this time. She thought a bit more, then brightened. "Man say you Rayder."

"Man? What man?"

She said something to the headman in her own tongue, then nodded. "Man who come . . ." She frowned. She pointed toward the east and swept her arm in a wide arc across the dome of the sky toward the west, then repeated that until she had shown the east to west rotation of the sun six times.

"Six days ago?" he asked.

She nodded.

"Do you know this man?"

"Not know. White man. Rich."

"Why did—"

The headman interrupted, saying something to the girl at considerable length and stopping several times to consult with the other members of the band before he was done. The girl listened patiently, then turned to Raider and struggled to explain it all in her feeble English.

The upshot of it was that a man had approached them. They did not know him, but he must at least have known about them. He knew about the Blue Walls station and told them to expect Raider there soon.

Yet six days ago, Raider realized, he himself had never heard of such a place as the Blue Walls on the old Mormon Road. Wasn't that downright interesting.

This white man would pay the Indians to wait at the Blue Walls and torment Raider for him. They were to be paid two rifles, ammunition, blankets, and knives. That much would have been a fortune to these desert people.

They were not supposed to kill him. That was what the Indian girl said, and Raider believed her. Aside from the fact that these people didn't seem at all the self-serving kind, and didn't seem the least lick like liars,

Raider knew damn good and well that if they'd wanted him dead he would *be* dead now. They were simply that good. So no, he didn't believe for a minute that they had agreed to kill him and then not done it.

Instead what they said the white man wanted of them was for the band to strand Raider out here and force him to die of thirst. Better yet, the man's aim was to make Raider panic and lose his mind, hopefully to the point of suicide.

That suggestion drew a derisive snort from Raider and a hearty bellylaugh from the Indians. Raider wasn't much the type for that sort of simple-minded shit, and by now the Indians knew that about as well as Raider did.

Still, that was what the SOB wanted done, and the band had taken the job in exchange for the promise of a treasure afterward.

Raider never did get it entirely clear through the fog of imprecise language, but apparently his assing around with them, sharing his food with the tribe when he might have been expected to hang on to it for himself, might have had something to do with their change of mind.

They'd known good and well that he would find the hidden water seep once they saw him setting up to wait for a bee or a bird to show him the way. Yet they hadn't tried to block him from the water then.

They were primitive, Raider decided, but honorable. A helluva lot more so than a good many white men he knew.

And for sure more so than whoever this white SOB was who wanted Raider dead.

He tried to get a description of the white man out of them, but the language problems made that impossible.

He had a vague sort of idea that the man they had talked to, the one who hired them to drive Raider to suicide, was *not* the tipster he'd seen back in Chloride when this whole thing got started.

But that was only an impression, not a fact.

On the other hand, Raider realized, that tipster back there spoke English just fine.

Raider would've been willing to make a sizable wager saying that he could get that scruffy tipster to give up everything he knew, everything he'd ever once known, and everything more that he ever hoped to know.

That fella in Chloride might become positively eager to spill whatever he knew once the questions were properly phrased.

"Thank you," Raider told the girl, who translated it on to the headman.

The headman touched his own chest, then reached over and laid the palm of his hand on Raider's chest. He nodded and smiled.

The girl didn't have to bother translating that gesture for Raider.

Raider smiled and left the circle around the embers of the fire. It was late and the meat was all gone, and the whole band looked to be pretty worn out by now.

This time Raider was allowed to return to his bed without company. The girl went off to share a blanket with one of the hunters who'd run the jackrabbit down earlier.

The headman, Raider noticed, seemed more interested in sleeping with the Winchester than with his wife. Which, everything considered, might not've been a bad choice. The rifle only smelled of light oil and gunpower.

Raider once again pulled the Stetson down over his eyes and this time was able to sleep the remainder of the night away without interruption.

CHAPTER TWENTY-SIX

The hike south to the Colorado River was long, hot, and tiring, but not really all that difficult once there was no one shooting at him.

Raider refused to take any of the drying mutton with him, leaving all that for the band of Indians—whose tribe he never had quite figured out even though he'd asked; the girl's answer had been another of those incomprehensible words that sounded like she was gagging on a chicken bone—and leaving the Winchester with them as well.

He did, though, carry a full canteen with him when he left, and the headman gifted him also with a disposable temporary canteen made from the bladder of the ewe Raider had shot. Two or three days at the most, Raider knew, and the bladder would rot enough to begin leaking. But then two or three days should see him safely back in Chloride unless he turned stupid and broke a leg or something on the way.

He reached the Colorado without incident and had to

climb down a sharp-walled bluff to reach the cool, swiftly flowing water.

First thing he did was to find a sand shelf in the backwash of an eddy and walked straight in waist deep. Then he sat down with a grin and let his dry and gritty pores become saturated with the cleansing river water.

He bathed, rested up a bit, and shot a disbelieving bobcat that roasted up nice and juicy for supper. Apparently there just weren't a helluva lot of humans seen in the neighborhood because the few animals he saw were much more curious about him than frightened.

From there, he figured, it would be another day or two downstream to the ford he'd crossed on his way north, then straight on to Chloride.

Raider was plenty anxious to get there now. But his desire had nothing to do with survival. Only with revenge.

The formerly friendly hotel clerk gave him a look of sharp suspicion when Raider lumbered into the lobby. But then, Raider conceded, he probably looked like hell warmed over. He was ragged and unshaven and stinking. His clothes were stained white with the salts from his own sweat, and nearly everything on him that was visible was coated with alkali dust.

"You still holdin' my room?" Raider demanded.

"Sir?"

"My room and my gear. You're still holding them for me, right?"

"I never . . ." Comprehension slowly dawned, and the clerk's eyes went wide. "Mr. Raider?"

"Ayuh."

"I thought . . . never mind what I thought, sir."

"Hell, I don't blame you. You got my things in storage somewhere?"

"Yes, sir." The response was quick this time.

"Then let's be draggin' it out and sent to a room for

me, hear? And a bath. Lordy, do I need a bath. You might call in the barber too and somebody to do some laundry for me."

"Yes, sir. Right away, sir." The clerk turned and snapped his fingers importantly in the direction of a bellboy who was barely big enough or old enough to lug a suitcase up a set of stairs. "Take care of the gentleman, Freddy. At once," he ordered.

The kid made a face, probably doubting that anyone who looked this shabby could afford much of a tip, but did what he was told anyway.

"One other thing," Raider said.

"Yes, sir?"

"I'd just as soon my name wasn't used about any of this. Just as soon nobody knew I was back in town."

"Sir?"

Raider smiled. "There's a friend I want to surprise, see."

"Oh. Very good, sir." The clerk smiled too.

Raider would have started his search for the tipster immediately and the hell with waiting to bathe, except that the Remington hadn't been cleaned for too many days and the cartridges in it had been immersed in the waters of the Colorado several times now.

Priorities and all that.

He smiled and signed the guest register anew and followed the bellboy up the stairs to a different hotel room than the one he remembered from before.

This evening was something he'd been looking forward to for what seemed a very long time now, and he was savoring his own anticipation of it.

CHAPTER TWENTY-SEVEN

A bath, clean clothes, and a shave can make all the difference in the way a man feels. Raider felt as renewed as if he'd had twelve hours sleep by the time he walked out of the hotel again.

More important than the way he felt, though, the Remington in his freshly cleaned and waxed holster leather was free of grit now, carefully oiled, and reloaded with cartridges from the supply that had stayed behind in the bottom of Raider's carpetbag while he made his wild goose journey to the Blue Walls.

If he found that weasely SOB . . . No, make that *when* he found the sonuvabitch.

Raider had no idea who the man was or where he lived. Possibly in Chloride, but probably not.

One bad thing about a place that existed mostly to cater to the needs of travelers was that strangers were no rarity here, and it was unlikely that anyone local would have found anything remarkable about the pudgy little tipster whose name Raider never had heard.

Direct questioning would probably only arouse suspicions, Raider decided. And the questions might get back to the tipster, if indeed he was still in town. Better, he decided, to search for the man himself with his eyes open and his mouth closed.

He ate supper in stages, a little at this restaurant and a little more at that cafe. The taste of greasy fried foods was wonderful after being so long without fats in his diet, but he was more interested in observing as many of Chloride's residents as possible than in satisfying his appetite. It was dinnertime, after all, and if the tipster was still in town he would have to eat too.

Raider began a slow stroll from one end of Chloride to the other and back again several times over, stopping in at cafes and saloons and every shop or store that was open for evening trade.

He saw one argument, two fistfights, and a kicking match between a mule and a draft horse—the mule won that one easily—but no sign of the tipster, damn it.

"Something I can he'p you with, neighbor?" a bartender at one of the seedier saloons asked.

"Just a beer, thanks." Raider laid a nickel on the counter to pay for the drink that he didn't want. It was, he figured, a price of admission, so to speak.

The bartender gave him a look of suspicion. "It ain't a beer you're looking for," he challenged.

"No?"

The barman's smile was tight-lipped, falling barely short of being a sneer. "Mister, this is the third time I seen you peep in here t'night, an' the first time you've come t' my bar. So no, I'd say it ain't no beer you're lookin' for."

His searching was becoming obvious then, at least to anyone who was reasonably observant. Raider didn't particularly care for that, but there wasn't much he could do about it except quit searching. And there was no way he was going to do that.

"Look, mister, I know what you're after," the barman ventured.

"You do?"

"Sure, man. It's natural, see. You don't hafta be shy about it."

"Do tell." Raider picked up the mug the man had set in front of him. He took a small sip off the top, which was mostly suds.

"I don't run no wimmin myself, see, but I know a lady. Has a nice clean place, she does. Best house in town." He chuckled. "Only place too, o' course, but clean. They'd treat y' right over there."

Raider affected what he hoped was a shy and hesitant look. If that was what the barman wanted to see, well, better to give it to him and avoid curiosity. Besides, he had been into every business in Chloride that he knew about and hadn't gotten a sniff of the tipster. Maybe the asshole was at this whorehouse Raider hadn't known about. Assuming the bastard still had some of his blood money to spend, the money he would have earned for sending Raider off to his death at the Blue Walls.

"Tell me about it," Raider invited.

"We got us a reform movement in town, see. Them damn Mormons. O' course they c'n afford t' sneer when it comes t' boughten pussy 'cause they keep s' damn many wives that they can have themselves some strange without never leavin' the fam'bly. Anyhow, see, that's why this place can't be open 'bout itself like a fella would expect. But it's a good place. You tell 'em Whit sent you an' they'll let y' in. Take nice care o' you. Be sure an' tell 'em who sent y' or they won't let y' in, though."

Raider smiled. Right. Sure. He'd never heard of a whorehouse yet that would turn a paying customer away. On the other hand, friendly ol' Whit here would be able to count on a finder's fee if Raider used his name. But then why not? Raider had nothing against free enterprise.

"You want to tell me where I can find this place, neighbor?"

"You bet," Whit said pleasantly. "Y' go out the door here an' turn left. T' the middle of the next block, see, an' there's a alley that runs between..."

Raider smiled and nodded and patiently took in the directions.

The tipster had to be some-damn-place, and Raider had already looked in every other public part of Chloride. Probably it would be a good idea to check out the whorehouse before he started barging into private homes looking for the son of a bitch who'd sent him into the desert to die.

CHAPTER TWENTY-EIGHT

The place was genuinely secretive about itself, tucked away at the back of a block of commercial buildings and with no lights or signs or any way of drawing attention to itself. If Raider hadn't gotten directions from that bartender he would never have been able to find it.

He found the door he'd been told to expect, having to feel his way along in the dark alley, and tried the knob. It turned under his hand, but the door wouldn't open. It was barred from inside.

Apparently someone posted close by heard the rattle of the doorknob, though. Raider barely had time to let go of the brass knob than a small square of lamplight appeared in front of his eyes as a peephole was swung open.

"Yes?" a deep voice asked.

"Just want t' come in," Raider said.

"Who sent you?"

Be damned. They really meant it. "Guy named Whit at the Green Bottle."

"All right, then." There was the sound of a bolt grating in metal, and the door was opened for him. The watchdog whose voice was so deep turned out to be a scrawny little rooster with bad teeth and a receding hairline. If this little fellow served as the bouncer, too, they would be in serious trouble in the event of a commotion.

"Thanks," Raider said politely. He stepped inside and removed his hat.

The room he found himself in was no more than a vestibule, just barely big enough to hold the watchman on his stool and with room enough for maybe two people to stand upright without gouging each other with their elbows. Closed doors led to left and right. Straight ahead there was a dark, narrow staircase.

"That way," the watchdog said, pointing toward the door on the left.

Raider thanked him again and let himself into a tidy parlor furnished in the flocked and brocaded style that was common in better houses anyplace in the country. Unlike the scarlet and gold color scheme that was normal, though, this place was decorated in soft, pale colors, perhaps making up for the fact that there were no windows in the room. It was no wonder Raider hadn't seen any light outside.

There were two customers in the parlor at the moment, each with a girl at his side. A third girl sat idle on a cream-colored sofa.

The place was nice enough but not fancy. Instead of the ball gowns worn by girls in the tiptop houses, these whores were lightly covered with thin cotton chemises and black stockings. A man didn't need much imagination to see what they were offering.

Not that Raider particularly cared. His immediate attention went to the customers. Both looked like drummers, unfortunately. There was no sign of the treacherous little tipster.

The girls were a sad mixture, dumpy, suety bodies

pocked heavily with pimples and caked powder. Flabby tits and meaty thighs.

They were available, but that was about the best that could be said for any of them.

Looking at them didn't give Raider a hard-on.

The girl who was unoccupied at the moment gave the new customer a dull, uninterested look. The other two were animated and lively. Raider guessed the third girl would pretend to be too if he showed some money.

"How may we help you, sir?" a voice asked from behind him.

He turned. This woman would be the madam, he figured. She was fully clothed in an old but decently cut gown and was smiling at him. She had entered the parlor after him, probably summoned by the watchdog from that closed door on the other side of the vestibule. He smiled back at her. "The obvious," he said.

"Of course, sir. A dollar short time, anything up to five dollars for, um, specialties, ten dollars for all night. What was it you had in mind, sir?"

Time, actually. Time enough to get a look at all the other customers in the place. But he couldn't exactly come right out and say so.

"Oh, I'd say prob'ly something in the five-dollar range," he told her.

"Very good, sir."

"But I'll want to get a look at all your girls so I can pick the one I like the best."

"Of course, sir."

"You do have more'n just these three, don't you?"

"I have seven ladies in residence at the moment, sir. Four happen to be occupied now. But I am sure you will find a companion suitable to your taste."

"Yeah, I'm sure I will."

"Would you care for a drink while you wait? A cigar? A snack, perhaps?"

"A beer'd be nice."

The madam led him to an overstuffed armchair, then went herself into a back room for the beer. She served it in a pilsner glass that was presented on a tray. And collected ten cents from him for a beer that was worth a nickel. The owner of this place had a good thing going, Raider decided, if they could get away with that kind of robbery.

"When you are ready to go upstairs, sir, just tell the lady of your choice."

"Thank you."

"Sir?"

"Mmm?"

"You've seen all the ladies by now, sir. I'll have to ask you to choose a companion or leave, please."

Raider frowned. If the tipster was in Chloride, damn it, this was probably the most likely place to find him. Customers were moving in and out at a steady pace despite the secrecy of it all, few of the men staying more than fifteen or twenty minutes before they were replaced in the parlor by later arrivals. Raider really didn't want to leave yet. He fished into his pocket for a half eagle, regretting now that he'd said he wanted the full treatment. If he didn't go through with it now the damned madam was likely to throw him out. A dollar quickie would have been better, though.

"And the lady of your choice, sir?"

There were five girls in the parlor at the moment. Raider didn't particularly fancy any of them. He pointed toward the least objectionable of the bunch, a redhead with pale skin and a too thin body. At least she wasn't an inch deep in old powder, and therefore looked to be cleaner than most.

"Lisa," the madam called. "Would you take care of the gentleman, please? Everything he wishes. Our five-dollar treatment, dear."

"Yes, ma'am." Lisa didn't sound especially happy

about the prospect of a five-dollar trick. By the time she reached Raider's side, though, she was smiling and vivacious, pawing at his biceps and oohing and ahing over them. "My, aren't you the handsome one," she exclaimed, practically overcome with the joy of being allowed to fuck such a fine and comely gentleman. "And so strong."

"Yeah, ain't I?" Raider growled.

"This way, sir," Lisa said gaily. She obviously hadn't paid the least bit of attention to his tone of voice. But then, hell, she probably was only marginally aware that he existed. Far as she would be concerned, the man known as Raider would only be another tumescent lump of flesh that had to be drained of its juices and then quickly exchanged for another just like it. To a girl like Lisa the paying customers would be just so many featureless cocks with no faces or personalities attached.

It shouldn't ought to be that way, Raider figured, but it always was.

He stood and allowed Lisa to lead him out of the parlor and up the narrow stairs.

CHAPTER TWENTY-NINE

By the time Raider had the door bolted and his coat off, Lisa was naked. She perched on the side of the hard, lumpy bed that was her workplace and quickly stripped away the black stockings. Her chemise already lay in a tangle at the foot of the mattress.

She wasn't really any better-looking without her clothes. Her tits were small but flaccid despite that. Most young women—he guessed Lisa was still in her twenties—with small breasts make up in firmness what they lack in size. Lisa's tits were like two dollops of pancake batter that weren't cooked yet; they flowed down her chest loosely, her nipples riding them like a pair of oversized raisins put there to decorate the pale batter.

Her belly showed the stretch marks of at least one birthing, and there was a dark, puckered scar marring her left hip.

Raider gave her credit for a degree of honesty, though. She was a sure-nuff redhead, the patch of bright color showing low as well as high.

She saw him looking at her and smiled. "Don't you worry, hon. I'm gonna make you feel so good you'll turn inside out."

He gave her a weak grin in return and resigned himself to going through with it. After all, he wanted an excuse to hang around and observe the customers a while longer tonight. This way he could claim he was resting and building up the strength to maybe take another walk up the stairs.

Lisa tossed the second stocking aside and padded barefoot across the small room to help him with his buttons. The bottoms of her feet were dark with grime from the uncarpeted floor, but otherwise she seemed clean enough. That was a relief.

"You just lay down, hon, and let Lisa take care of everything."

She turned to the nightstand and tipped a little water from the pitcher into an enameled basin, then dipped a cloth into it and without ceremony picked up his cock—damn thing wasn't cooperating much; it was still limp—and rinsed it off. The water was cold and did nothing to make him more interested in what she was doing.

She bent down to give it a playful kiss and a pat—that was better—then let go of it so she could wash herself with the same wet rag. She wadded the cloth into a lump and scrubbed her pussy as vigorously as if she'd been scouring a pot. Raider had to wonder if there was any feeling left at all down there, the way she was treating it. Like it was an inanimate object, actually.

"There, hon. All sweet an' clean. Roll over now. On your tummy. That's better."

Five dollars and she wanted him face-down? He did what she asked, though. It seemed easier than trying to think up desires that he didn't really have at this particular moment.

"You just close your eyes, hon, and enjoy what Lisa's gonna give you."

Raider relaxed and let his eyes sag shut. He was mighty tired, after all. If nothing else he'd be able to get a ten-minute snooze for his five dollars.

He felt a whisper-light touch between his shoulder blades. Then another on the back of his neck.

Her hair, he decided. She'd unpinned her hair and let it fall free. That had to be what he was feeling there so light and soft.

Warm, though. Now that he was paying some mind to it, he realized that the feather-tip touch was warm, and that wasn't what you'd expect from a wisp of hair.

Moist, too. Wherever she'd just been he could feel a cool, almost chilly aftertouch as the wetness she left behind commenced to evaporate.

He grunted as recognition came to him. It wasn't her hair she was trailing over his neck and shoulders but the tip of her tongue, touched down so light he could scarcely feel it. Be damned.

He smiled just a little.

Lisa shifted on the bed beside him. He could feel the warmth of her thigh soft against his hip when she changed positions.

She licked the pads of hard muscle below his shoulders, and now he could feel gentle, fluid heat against his lower back, too. It took him a moment to work that one out. While she licked him she was dragging the tips of her nipples over him too.

He wriggled just a little and became conscious that while he wasn't looking he'd somehow gone and worked up a hard-on. So much for real desire having anything to do with it. The plain and simple fact was that once a willing female set about giving a fella a bath with her tongue, he wasn't going to stay soft and uninterested very long unless he happened already to be pretty thoroughly dead.

Lisa was slow and thorough and patient about what she was doing.

She started high on his back and covered every square inch of skin she could reach. Up onto the nape of his neck and around to each ear, then back again and downward.

She traced the ridges of his spine with her tongue and like to drove him into a fit when she got to his sides just above waist level. That tickled so bad it didn't much feel good.

Apparently she felt the reaction in his squirming because she didn't stay there long. Instead she turned half around again, this time lying close against him and beginning to use her hands as well as her tongue.

She licked and nibbled the cheeks of his ass, then burrowed her face into his crack and lightly, teasingly circled her tongue around and around his hole. Licking, pausing, now and then probing.

Hadn't been *interested*? Shee-it. Raider was so interested by now that he was vibrating. He had a hard-on that would probably spear clean through a sheet of marble without so much as bending.

He moaned and held himself tense as the pink, pointy tip of Lisa's tongue probed and flickered.

"Relax, hon. I can't get down in here nice if you tighten up on me like that."

He tried, but it damn sure wasn't easy.

After a bit Lisa left that highly enjoyable pursuit and roamed southward again with that ever-busy tongue of hers.

She wasn't much for skipping over anything and moving along to the more interesting parts. She was gonna cover it all. Down first one leg and then the other. The soles of his feet and between his toes. She lay on top of him head to foot and back to belly and sucked on his toes one by one by one.

Raider wasn't sure, but he thought the top of his head just might fly off and splatter against the wall.

She shifted off him.

"Roll over now, hon. On your back, please. That's better."

He could see her now. She looked businesslike and serious about what she was doing.

Hell, that was all right. Give sensations like this and she was entitled to look like a damn harpy for all he cared. A Medusa with a nest of snakes for hair would be just fine if this was what she was up to. Shee-oot.

"Relax now, hon. Lisa knows what she's doing."

Raider had to agree with that assessment, thank you.

"Close your eyes, hon. It's better if you close your eyes."

He closed his eyes.

She started right in where she'd just left off, sucking on his toes and licking his feet. Up across the ankles and onto his legs again.

Ah, *now* she was getting to the good part.

Except that she wasn't.

The damn girl skipped right over a hard-on that was threatening to explode without ever once being touched.

She jumped from his thighs up to his head and commenced licking his forehead. Ran her tongue into his ears and around them. Over his eyes and even inside his nostrils. He shivered and tried to turn his head away.

"Huh-uh," she cautioned. "Let me."

He let her. He took a handful of tit so soft and fluid it flowed like warm honey through his fingers and let her do what she knew how to do so damn well.

She licked his cheeks and traced the line of his jaw and his chin but was careful to avoid coming near to his mouth. That simply wasn't done.

She laved his neck with the warm moisture of her tongue and down onto his chest. She stopped awhile at his nipples, and Raider decided maybe she'd been right after all. There hadn't been any need to hurry this procedure.

Then down onto his belly, into his navel—that tickled

too, the sensation of it somehow tingling deep inside his belly and all the way down into his legs—and finally, *finally* down to his balls.

His nuts were swollen and positively painful by now, but did that stop Lisa or so much as speed her up? Of course not. He should've known better than to hope for it.

By now he wanted to grab the back of her head and jam her face over his cock. He settled for taking a fistful of sheet with each hand and squeezing hard as he could to grip the cloth. It was a good thing she'd moved down to where he wasn't holding onto her tit anymore or she would've been screaming.

Lisa still wouldn't shortcut the inch-by-inch thoroughness of the five-dollar special.

She nuzzled in between his legs and licked his balls and moved on to the tender, sensitive flesh between his scrotum and his ass, then just as slowly moved back again.

Finally, damn it, she reached the base of his cock and licked it. Then higher. Higher still.

Raider was sure he was going to squirt the ceiling if she didn't hurry up.

She ran her tongue around and around the head of his cock.

And at last, mercifully, covered it with her lips.

Just barely, though. Just at the very tip.

She sucked, and her hands cupped and warmed his balls.

He didn't *need* any more arousal, damn it.

What he needed now was *release*.

This felt so good it hurt.

He reached up and put a hand on the back of her head. It was all he could do to keep himself from grabbing hold and hurting her.

He felt the movement as she nodded, understanding

what he needed. As if there could've been any doubt, damn her.

She dipped her head lower. Enveloping him. Taking him now into her mouth. Deep and then deeper and on into her throat. Sucking hard now and squeezing his balls just short of serious pain.

That one hot, deep penetration was all it took. Raider'd been ready for ten minutes. Now he was fixing to bust.

He arched his back in an involuntary convulsion, and a ragged, gasping grunt tore out of his throat as all that pent up heat and need gushed out of him and into her.

It went on and on for almost forever, and he was in no hurry for it to end now that it was started.

Damn!

Lisa stayed with him patiently until the last drop oozed out.

Then she sat up as a matter-of-fact as if she'd just finished tasting a new recipe and covered her mouth with a washcloth that she produced from somewhere. She spit his come into it and wiped her lips and chin and crawled off the foot of the bed to reach for her stockings and chemise.

Ceremonious she was not. Not even particularly friendly.

But good? Lordy. He shivered and rolled onto his side. He felt like she'd emptied him of a month's supply of seed. Next month's, at that.

Not that he was complaining.

Five dollars? The damn girl was a bargain at that rate.

He actually felt weak-kneed and shaky when he stood to pull his jeans on.

And to think that he hadn't been interested when he walked up those stairs. Dummy.

Lisa sat with a bored look on her face while Raider finished dressing. No offer to help with the buttons this time.

But no complaints. No sir, not one.

The only possible doubt he had right now was whether he could keep a straight face when he told the madam that he wanted to hang around the parlor a while longer to see if he'd be up to seconds. Hell, he doubted that a stud horse could be up to seconds after a go-round like this one.

He stamped his feet to settle them comfortably inside his boots and made sure the Remington was riding where it ought to, then picked up his Stetson.

Without another word Lisa nodded and led the way down the stairs to the parlor again.

CHAPTER THIRTY

This was a night damned well spent. And not because of Lisa either. He corrected that. Not *just* because of Lisa.

The pudgy little son of a bitch from the Blue Walls walked in around two or three in the morning.

Raider was sitting in the parlor with a warm, barely tasted beer beside him—it still rankled that the lousy beer cost so much here—when the madam opened the vestibule door and beckoned for Lisa to join her.

Over her shoulder Raider could see the cloth cap and the detestable face that he remembered so well.

The SOB must be a regular, Raider guessed, and his preference was for the redhead. Raider could understand that, all right. The coincidence of it was almost amusing. But probably to be expected. Lisa'd been up the stairs and back down again twice since Raider finished with her—or to be more honest about it, since she finished with Raider—and routinely stayed up there longer than any of the other whores did. The girl was a regular gold mine for whoever owned the house.

Raider wondered if the tipster was planning to spend five dollars of his blood money. The blood money he would've collected for a certain Pinkerton operative's death.

For what he and somebody else *thought* would be Raider's death, anyhow.

A grim smile thinned Raider's lips, and he picked up the beer and nursed another small sip from it as Lisa and the madam disappeared into the vestibule with the fat client.

There was no sense in causing a ruckus inside the whorehouse, Raider realized.

Aside from it being impolite, if the fat man was indeed a regular here, the employees were likely to jump to his defense without bothering to ask questions.

Raider could live with the thought of injuring civilians in exchange for getting to this particular asshole, but he would prefer for it to be otherwise.

And the place was protected by somewhat more than the scrawny little doorman on his stool. While Raider had been watching and pretending—but not having to pretend all that much by now—the possibility of a renewed interest in the merchandise, he'd several times seen the bouncer of the house.

The guy was too big to take on with anything less than a singletree to hit him with. And at that, a large-bore revolver would probably be a better idea.

Raider had seen ox sheds that were smaller. Not the oxen, mind, but the barns to keep 'em in.

So a certain amount of privacy in this matter seemed definitely in order here.

He gave Lisa and the fat man time to clear the stairs and lock themselves inside the room Raider remembered right well, then took another swallow of the tepid beer and picked up his Stetson.

"Leaving?" the doorman with the deep voice asked.

"Gotta find an outhouse," Raider explained.

"There isn't one in this whole block. Not that just anybody can use. Private, you know. If all you gotta do is piss, use the alley."

"An' if I don't?"

The doorman gave him directions.

"Maybe I'll be back."

The doorman shrugged. He couldn't have cared less.

The night air even inside the dark alley felt cool and smelled clean after the odors indoors. Raider hadn't been consciously aware of them while he was in the parlor, but the place smelled of sweat and perfume and stale smoke. The alley was better.

He waited until the whorehouse door closed behind him, then felt his way through the alley toward the street. The ground was oddly free of litter. But then it saw considerably more traffic through it than an alley was normally intended for.

There were no niches conveniently placed where a man could hide—possibly that was deliberate, a service provided for the protection of the customers—and if he waited between the whorehouse and the street he would be silhouetted against the paler gray darkness of the street. The shadows inside the alley were stygian.

He retraced his way to the closed and bolted doorway without finding anyplace suitable to waylay someone departing from the house of pleasures.

There were times when other people's thoughtful efficiency was downright annoying.

He settled finally for taking a seat on a bench set against the front of a store that adjoined the alley mouth.

He didn't know for sure if there was another way in and out of the alley, but this would have to do.

Raider made himself comfortable on the bench and settled in to wait for the Blue Walls tipster to emerge.

CHAPTER THIRTY-ONE

The cloth cap was recognizable even from behind. Raider left the bench and in four swift strides was close behind the little son of a bitch who had tried to send him to his death.

"Evenin'," he said pleasantly.

"Good evening, I..." The fat man's eyes went wide and his face pale as recognition flooded through him.

Raider was a head taller than the tipster and stood now looming dark and grim over him.

"I, uh... I guess you've come to pay me my reward money, right?"

Raider's teeth bared. But he wasn't smiling. "Guess again."

"Look, I... I heard that Dial didn't go to the Walls after all. Maybe I steered you wrong about that."

The man was visibly trembling.

"Let's go for a walk, you an' me," Raider suggested.

"Really I, uh, can't. Right now. But I could meet you

tomorrow. We could talk then. I, uh, have an appointment now. I couldn't possibly miss it."

"Want to place a bet on that?" Raider didn't have enough respect for this miserable little weasel to come at him with a gun already in hand. Instead he poked the trembling, sweating little man in the ribs with a thumbnail.

The fellow damn near passed out. To him the prod must certainly have felt like a revolver muzzle.

"Anything you say, Mr. Raider. Anything at all."

"Somehow I figured you'd want to help."

"Yessir, absolutely, sir, whatever you say, sir."

"We'll take a little walk out in the country," Raider suggested.

"Yessir, that sounds fine."

"Down the street and straight on out of town. I'll tell you where to stop."

"Yes, sir, Mr. Raider."

The little man tugged a kerchief out of his coat pocket and mopped his forehead and neck, then stumbled off the sidewalk and onto the hard-baked soil of the street. Every second or third step he looked fearfully over his shoulder.

If he was hoping that the next glance would find him alone in the night, he was sadly disappointed.

"Far enough," Raider said when they were a good quarter mile past the last buildings of Chloride.

The tipster stopped and turned. His face was pasty white in the moonlight, and the front of his trousers was stained dark where he'd wet himself.

Raider hauled the big Remington from his holster, the tipster's eyes locked on it every inch of the way.

He took his time about cocking the revolver, giving the guy plenty of time to stare at it.

Then Raider reached forward with his free hand and pulled at the waistband of the sweaty bastard's trousers.

The tipster wore suspenders but no belt, so the cloth pulled freely away from his belly.

With a wolfish grin, Raider shoved the barrel of the cocked Remington inside the front of the tipster's britches.

"Faint on me now, mister, and you'll pull on my hand when you fall. I figure you can guess what that'd do when the gun goes off, mmm?"

"Jesus, mister. Oh, Jesus. Don't..." He squirmed and wriggled but did *not* pull away.

"Up to you," Raider suggested, "how much you want to tell me. Up to me if I think it's enough to keep me from pulling this trigger."

"You can't... you wouldn't..."

"If you believe that, why, you're sure entitled to call my bluff, mister. All you gotta do is square them shoulders of yours and tell me I ain't man enough to blow your nuts to a red, wet mush. If that's what you believe, that is."

"Please, I... anything. Honest, Mr. Raider. I'll tell you anything you want to know. Just... take the gun away? Please?"

"When I've decided which way I want to do this," Raider agreed. He waggled the barrel back and forth a bit.

"God, Mr. Raider, please, I... just listen to me..."

"Uh-huh. I think that's what we come out here for. You talk; I'll listen. Then we'll see what happens next."

The tipster wiped his forehead again, very careful in his movements lest he jar Raider's hand.

"It's like this, Mr. Raider..."

Raider frowned. The question, of course, wasn't whether the guy had talked enough. It was whether all or even any of it had been the truth.

The tipster's name was Buddy Bennett. And he didn't know a damn thing more about Jonas Dial than the man's name. He had never seen Dial nor so much as heard of the wanted man until he was given the tale that he was supposed to relate to Raider. Jonas Dial might be holed up anywhere from Canada to Guatemala for all Buddy Bennett knew.

Bennett did know about the Blue Walls, though, because he used to work there. He tended the livestock, helped the station keeper change the hitches, did whatever odd jobs had been required around the place until the stage company folded and went out of business, done under by railroads and better coach routes.

No, there never had been any water at the Blue Walls. They'd tried but never located water there. Water had to be hauled in in tank trailers, and all the hay and grain they needed too. The expense of maintaining the station like that had contributed to the company's failure.

No, Bennett didn't know anything about any Indians. Except that there were supposed to be some. The man who'd hired him had set all that up. Raider wasn't sure if he should believe that denial or not. Bennett, after all, was the one who had some experience in that country. Not the other man.

Bennett claimed he'd been hired by a man who called himself Elbert Smith, Jr. "But I overheard one time, Mr. Raider, when he bumped into somebody who acted like they knew Smith. Guy said, 'Hello, Billy' or 'howdy, Billy,' something like that. Smith glanced at him an' looked away real quick. Made out like he'd not seen this fella before, but I could see that they knew each other. The other fella got this embarrassed look about him and hurried off someplace else. I don't know if they got together after that or not."

"Billy," Raider repeated. The name Elbert Smith, Jr., told him nothing. And a man once known as Billy could be any one of half a thousand men.

"Yes, sir, that's what I heard him called. But just that one time, by accident like."

Smith, or Billy, was medium tall, dark hair, dark eyes, bushy beard, a little heavyset. Real pale, Bennett said. No scars or distinguishing marks on him.

The description could have fit nearly anyone.

Bennett and Smith met when Smith was drunk and Bennett tried to roll him for his pocket money. Except Smith hadn't been drunk enough.

"He had a gun, Smith did. Me, I never carry one. I don't like guns, Mr. Raider." He cast his gaze significantly low and squirmed again. Raider's Remington was still stuffed inside the front of Bennett's trousers. Raider figured it could just as well stay where it was for the time being.

"Anyhow, see, he pointed this gun at me. Then he laughed and said he wasn't gonna shoot, that he didn't blame me for trying to pick up a little money when I was down and out. He put the gun back in his pocket and said he'd buy me a drink. We got to talking after that. Talked a lot, about all kinds of things. And when I mentioned that I hadn't had a real good job since the stage line folded and told him about the Blue Walls station, that's when he got kinda interested and started wanting to know more about it. Said it was the sort of place he'd been looking for. Wanted to know all about it. He even rented horses and the two of us rode out there."

"How long ago?" Raider asked. It was clear already that this setup had taken a while to develop.

Bennett shrugged. "I dunno. A month? Maybe that."

"A month." Raider scratched the side of his nose. When he moved the Remington must have wiggled again, because Bennett twitched and moaned.

"I don't know for certain sure how long it was," Bennett bawled. "I swear that I don't."

"Go on," Raider ordered. He was thinking, though, that a month ago there was no way in hell anyone could have predicted that he was going to be sent to Chloride, Arizona Territory.

Unless, of course, that someone had a hand in sending him there.

"That's most of it, Mr. Raider. I swear that it is. Smith and me went out and I showed him where the Blue Walls was. Then we came back here and he paid me some money to live on and went away for a while. When he came back he told me that you'd be coming and what I was to do. Which you already know about."

Raider grunted. He knew, all right.

"All I done, Mr. Raider, is what this Smith fella paid me to do. I never meant to hurt you. Honest. I thought it was just a joke he was playing on you."

Bennett gave Raider a trembly, weak-lipped smile.

The dumb son of a bitch surely didn't think he was going to believe that, Raider thought. A joke? Sure. Some joke. And he'd already admitted to knowing there were going to be some Indians involved. Surely had to know that the whole idea was to get Raider to thirst to death in the desert. Hell, some men probably would've panicked and died out there. A man like Buddy Bennett, for instance.

Raider scowled and shoved the Remington forward an inch or so.

"Don't *do* that," Bennett squealed.

"I'll do a hell of a lot worse if it pleases me, asshole."

"Yessir," Bennett said contritely. He licked his lips and shivered.

"What are you supposed to do now?" Raider demanded.

"I . . . oh, God, I don't wanta have to tell you this."

"Your choice," Raider agreed. He gave the revolver a nudge as if pulling the trigger.

"Wait!" Bennett yelped. "Wait, I . . . I'll tell you."

"Whatever you prefer."

"I'm . . . I'm supposed to wait a week, Mr. Raider,

after you left for the Blue Walls, then ride up to the crossing on the Colorado. I'm supposed to meet the Indians there and . . . and . . . oh, Jesus, don't make me say this part. Please don't."

"Hell, I'm not making you say none of this shit. You got a clear choice. Still have." He pushed on the butt of the gun again.

"I'm supposed to meet these Indians and collect . . . something from them."

"Something?"

"Your, uh, head." He mopped his forehead again but might not have bothered. He was as sweaty when he was done as before he started.

"You said something about thinking the whole thing was a joke? You think it's funny, Bennett?"

"Jesus, Mr. Raider, I just didn't . . . I didn't want to have to say that part, that's all. Out loud, like."

"Tell me what you're supposed to do once you have my head, Bennett."

"I'm supposed . . . supposed to carry it with me, and take the Indians along too, and give it to Mr. Smith. Then he's supposed to pay me some more and pay the Indians whatever he promised them."

"Where is this meeting supposed to take place?" Raider asked softly.

"The . . . the old Mormon Fort, Mr. Raider. At the Meadows. Las Vegas, some call it. It was another stop on the stage line. But it's been abandoned for years too."

"Another dry station?"

"No, sir. Las Vegas has good water and grass around it. That's why they call it that. Nothing there now but travelers stopping for the night now and then."

"And Mr. Elbert Smith, Jr., is gonna meet you there?"

"Yessir, just like I said. I was gonna leave day after tomorrow to find them Indians and, uh, do what I was told."

Raider grunted. "I'm probably going to want to kill you anyway, Bennett," he said. "But I might not. I haven't decided yet."

"Please, sir, I—"

"Shut up, Bennett."

Bennett clamped his mouth shut instantly.

"First I want to see just how much of what you say is lies, and—"

"I swear to you, Mr. Raider, that—"

"Shut up, Bennett."

"Yessir."

"Instead of you going to meet those Indians and collect my head in a poke, Bennett, you and me are going to take a ride to this Las Vegas place and talk to Mr. Smith. I'll let him tell me if you're a truthful man or not."

"God, Mr. Raider, you can't—"

"Bennett, I do admire a man with the courage to make the decision you are."

"No! I didn't mean *that*, Mr. Raider."

"Then you think it would be a good idea for the two of us to ride together so you can introduce me to your friend Smith?" He didn't honestly want to shoot Bennett down in cold blood. But he certainly wasn't going to turn the little prick loose either. If nothing else, he wanted Bennett where he could lay hands on the little SOB, just in case more of the story was lies than Raider already suspected. There were sure to be some lies mixed in there. Raider wanted to know how much truth was included before he made up his mind what to do with Buddy Bennett.

"Yes, sir. Yes, sir, I think that would be a *fine* thing for us to do, sir."

"Mind now, Bennett, I still might decide to shoot your nuts off. I'll let you know when I see how close your story checks out. Meantime, not that I don't trust you of course, but in the meantime I think you'd best turn around so I can snap some cuffs on your wrists." He withdrew the snout of the Remington from inside Bennett's britches. He was going to have to clean the revolver again now, though. Bennett would've pissed all over it.

Buddy Bennett seemed right happy to turn his back and accept the handcuffs.

CHAPTER THIRTY-TWO

Whoever Elbert Smith, Jr./used-to-be-Billy was, he seemed to be mighty well bankrolled for his murderous game.

Raider took the precaution of emptying Buddy Bennett's pockets when they got back to the hotel. Bennett carried nothing more lethal than a straight pin—useful for marking cards but stupid because the method was so easily detectable by other players at the table—but he still had nearly two hundred dollars left on him. And that was after living it up for at least the better part of a week. Raider was impressed. Smith/Billy was forking out cash in large quantities in exchange for a head that Raider would just as soon he never collected.

But who was this son of a bitch?

Nothing Bennett said gave any hints.

Somebody with a mighty serious hard-on for Raider, that was sure.

Raider shrugged and got a second set of steel cuffs from his bag.

"Lie down there," he ordered.

"You aren't gonna . . . ?"

"Naw, that'd make a mess on the floor. Wouldn't be fair to the nice folks at the hotel here. If I do decide to kill you, I'll take you outside so it won't be so much trouble getting rid of the blood. Most of it sinks into the ground, you know. Then all you gotta do is kick a little loose dirt over the spot."

Bennett swallowed and looked like he wanted to throw up. "You shouldn't tease me, Mr. Raider."

"I ain't teasing."

Bennett dropped to the floor in a hurry.

Raider used one pair of cuffs on Bennett's ankles, linking them over the bed frame so the man was secured there. Then he unlocked the set already on the fat man's wrists and secured those over the bed frame too. Bennett wasn't going anywhere in the night, what little was left of it, without Raider knowing.

"I won't give you no trouble, Mr. Raider. You have my word on it."

"Thank you, Bennett. That does make me feel easier in my mind."

Bennett turned his face away and offered no complaints about what was undoubtedly a most uncomfortable sleeping position.

Raider kicked his boots off and hung the holstered Remington on the bedpost—not on the same side as where he had tethered his prisoner, though—and lay down.

He was half asleep when something flickered through his thoughts.

His eyes snapped open, and he tried to recapture whatever the thought had been.

Something Bennett had said? Something about Smith/Billy?

Whatever it was, damn it, it had fled before he could drag it up onto the surface of his thoughts.

He closed his eyes again and let sleep take him.

• • •

The telegraph office was open when Raider woke up. In fact if it had shut down over the lunch hour it would have been open and then closed again. It was past noon by the time Raider dragged Bennett with him into the street.

Passers-by gave the handcuffed prisoner curious looks, but no one approached the pair, and certainly no one challenged Raider's authority to be walking the streets of Chloride with a man in irons.

"Yes, sir?" the telegraph clerk asked when Raider and company stepped inside.

"My name's Raider. With the Pinkerton Agency. Would you happen to have any messages for me?"

The clerk frowned. "Nothing recent, Mr. Raider. But wait a second. I think . . . let me look at something here." He turned and rooted through a pile of papers in a pigeonhole on the side of his rolltop desk. "Yes, sir, this is addressed to you, but it's been sitting here the better part of a week now."

Raider accepted the message form and quickly scanned it.

That was all it took. He didn't need a second reading to confirm what he'd already suspected last night.

WHY MEET CLIENT PHIPPS STOP NOT YOUR ASSIGNMENT STOP WHY YOU NOT ARKANSAS STOP CONTACT IMMEDIATELY IMPERATIVE.

"I'm not Arkansas because I'm Raider," he mumbled.

"Pardon me?"

"Nothing. Sorry." He gave the clerk a smile and led Bennett out in search of someplace that might still be willing to serve a breakfast. His stomach didn't feel up to a greasy lunch yet.

The telegraph message from Chicago confirmed it.

Smith/Billy faked the Phipps assignment to get Raider here. Raider *in particular*, not just the next handy Pinkerton operative.

How Smith/Billy might have learned about Phipps . . . hell, maybe Raider could ask him directly. Something like that probably wouldn't be an impossible task, though, if a man was determined to ferret out some information. Sit down with a Pinkerton operative and chat him up. Talk about nuisance cases. Someone was sure to mention Phipps and his fruitless but stubborn search, and never give thought to the idea that he was being pumped for deadly information when he talked about it. Find out where Raider was by the same method.

Then get a message off to Raider ordering him to Chloride to work on the Phipps case.

Hell, that would be all that was necessary.

No wonder Wagner was confused when Raider's message from Arizona Territory came in saying he would be unable to meet Phipps.

As far as the head office knew, he wasn't supposed to meet Phipps anyplace.

As for the Arkansas assignment, that message must have come in after Raider was already long gone from where Wagner and Allan Pinkerton expected to find him.

Raider frowned. He wasn't going to respond to that "imperative" demand that he contact them. Not quite yet. They would want explanations. Then bitch about the cost of the telegrams if he did try to explain it all.

No, he'd been out of touch this long. Another few days wasn't really going to matter.

Better, he decided, to keep one eye on Bennett and the other looking for Elbert Smith, Jr./good-ol'-Billy.

Soon as he'd eaten, he figured, he could start arranging transportation to this Las Vegas place.

And woe unto that poor sad sonuvabitch Bennett if there wasn't any Smith/Billy waiting there to collect a head.

CHAPTER THIRTY-THREE

From Chloride to Las Vegas should have been a day and a half, two days taking it easy. Raider and Buddy Bennett made it in one long push by leaving early and leading spare horses.

Raider had no idea who would end up paying for all the horseflesh he was using up lately, but then he didn't much give a shit either. Elbert Smith, Jr./sometimes Billy wanted his fucking *head*. And not as some idle figure of speech either. He wanted the thing in a bag. On a platter? Raider asked. No, Bennett assured him, Elbert Smith hadn't said anything about a platter. Just that he should bring the head with him when he came.

Somehow that didn't make Raider feel the least bit more charitable toward Mr. Smith.

There was good road to travel to the Colorado River and beyond it, and a ferry there so they could cross dry and comfortable.

Hours beyond the river crossing they cut the old but still distinct wheel ruts that Bennett said had been the

Mormon Road, the same seldom used road that the Blue Walls straddled a good many miles to the north and east from Las Vegas.

"Good thing I know I can trust you to guide me right where I want to go," Raider observed as he reined his horse and the others onto the dry road. Bennett's and both spare horses were trotting on lead ropes while Raider handled the reins for all of them.

"You can trust me, Mr. Raider," Bennett assured him.

Raider smiled. "'Course I can, Bennett. An' we both know why."

Buddy Bennett was a long way from forgetting the feel of Raider's big Remington against his cods. Raider suspected if the man lived another hundred years, that was one memory that would still be fresh in his mind.

"I wish you wouldn't say stuff like that, Mr. Raider."

"Shut up, Bennett."

"Yes, sir."

They traveled on into the afternoon, stopped for a cold lunch in the shade of a cloud no bigger than a bandana—there wasn't anything else for miles around that would have created any more shade than that—and rode on again after switching saddles and mounts for the fourth time.

"It isn't far now," Bennett assured him just before dusk. "But you gotta remember, Mr. Raider, that he won't be expecting me there for another few days. I mean, I'm still supposed to be up by the Blue Walls meeting them Indians and bringing them down. He won't know when to meet me, so he might not be there yet."

"You sound like you might be setting me up for disappointment, Bennett. I don't think I'd like that."

Bennett went pale and protested his innocence until Raider was sick of listening to him whine about it.

"I'm not ready to shoot you yet, Bennett, but I might ride happier if I stuffed a gag down your throat."

Bennett rode quiet after that.

Raider could see the place called the Meadows well before they reached it. There was a swath of cool green grass spread over the ground in the midst of the desert here, and a narrow trickle of sweet water running through it.

Beside some dying cottonwoods there were some tumbledown adobe buildings surrounded by the remains of an adobe wall.

"That's the Mormon Fort," Bennett offered.

By now there was so little left of the wall that Raider would have taken it for a corral instead of a fortress, but as they came nearer he could see that the remaining buildings had gun ports designed to command a field of fire outside the walls, and a ditch had been dug around the foundations to keep attackers from reaching the gun ports to shoot into them.

There were no horses or mules in sight at the moment, but ash rings and manure piles and wheel tracks showed that the buildings were used for temporary refuge every so often. Unlike Blue Walls, this Mormon Fort wasn't far off the normal routes of travel.

"He ain't here yet," Bennett said, "but he'll be along soon. You can count on that, Mr. Raider. I swear I haven't lied to you."

The little fat man was sweating and shaking so bad Raider thought he was going to fall out of his saddle.

Raider grunted and dismounted. He took Bennett by the belt and hauled him off the horse, then motioned him to a seat on the ground before he led the horses into a corner that had been closed off with adobe rubble to form a makeshift corral enclosure.

Raider didn't expect Bennett would try to run while his hands were cuffed behind his back. But he wasn't going to count on that. The tubby tipster was too clumsy to get to his feet without assistance while he was cuffed, so Raider felt better about having him on the ground while the camp chores were tended to.

"We'll wait, Bennett," Raider said when he carried their gear back and started toward the best-looking of the remaining buildings. "Then we'll see if you've been lying to me or not."

"Mr. Raider, I swear—"

"Shut up, Bennett."

Raider was standing looking down at Buddy Bennett. His back was to the derelict buildings.

He heard the crunch of a boot sole on gravel and spun.

A huge man wearing a thick, black beard stood in the sagging doorway of the largest building.

He had a rifle in his hands.

Raider swore. He was carrying both their bedrolls, one in each hand. He threw the sougan in his left hand high into the air as a distraction and dropped the other so he could palm the Remington.

It wasn't the fastest draw he'd ever made. But that wasn't for the lack of trying.

Damn it.

CHAPTER THIRTY-FOUR

"Whoa, neighbor. I ain't hostile." The big man smiled and held his rifle harmlessly out to the side to demonstrate that he wasn't wanting to shoot.

"You startled me," Raider said. The Remington was cocked and pointing toward the big fellow's middle.

"Y'know, I kinda figured that," he agreed.

Raider squinted at the man for a moment. He was positive he'd never seen this man before in his life.

And Bennett had said something about Smith/Billy being of middlin' size. Bearded, true, but not big. This man was half a mountain.

"You want to hold your fire, little fellow, while I set Bessie aside?"

Little fellow. There weren't a hell of a lot of men around who could call Raider that and mean it. This one qualified.

"Sorry." Raider let the hammer down on the Remington and dropped it into his holster while the man in the doorway gingerly set his rifle down. "Could we start over, mister?"

The big man laughed and nodded. "Name's Loon Michaels."

Raider introduced himself but didn't bother giving any explanations about Bennett, who still lay handcuffed in the dirt.

He couldn't help asking, "Loon, you say?"

Michaels chuckled agreeably and explained, "Loon 'cause everybody says I'm loony. I got me a gut feeling that there's gold waiting to be found in this country. That's what I'm doing here. Prospecting for it. I'll find it, too. Mark my words that I will. There's gold somewhere around here, and Loon Michaels is gonna be the man to find it."

"I wish you luck, Mr. Michaels."

"Just Loon. I don't mind the name."

"Fair enough."

"Got some coffee I can share," Michaels offered. "Was just fixing to start me a fire and boil a pot. You're welcome to whatever I got. Best place to sleep at the fort here is in this building. Only one that has all its roof yet. Or does either of you fellas object to sharing quarters with a canary?"

"Not so long as it doesn't step on me," Raider said.

Bennett craned his neck and gave Raider an odd look. "Step on you? Why would you care if a canary stepped on you?"

Michaels laughed and came out to help Raider gather up their gear. Raider dragged Bennett onto his feet and gave him a push toward the doorway.

"You a lawman, Raider?" Michaels asked.

"Pinkerton."

"Close enough. What's his problem?" Michaels inclined his head toward Bennett's back, seemingly quite willing to discuss the fat little tipster as openly as if Bennett weren't there listening.

"Tried to make himself out a killer," Raider said. "Not very good at it though."

"Come here for a tree to hang him from, did you?"

"No, just passing through."

Loon Michaels looked disappointed. But only mildly so.

Bennett was first inside the old fort. He stopped and stared. "But I thought you said—"

"Desert canary," Michaels told him. "You know. Hee-haw, hee-haw."

"Oh."

Michaels winked at Raider and carried the bedrolls to a spot across the room from his burro.

The prospector, Raider saw, traveled with a lean and spartan camp setup. One pot, a few blankets, a few bags holding this or that. Most of his gear seemed to be rock hammers and bottles of chemicals held gently in wooden racks that were designed specifically for the purpose of protecting them. Loon Michaels was called loony, maybe, and followed a gut-level hunch to be concentrating on this barren country, but he was sharp enough to test his rock samples with modern, efficient chemicals. Maybe Loon wasn't completely loony after all. Raider wished him well in his search.

"Don't have any meat to share," Michaels said. "Been quite a while since I seen anybody else's smoke."

"That's all right. We have more than enough. Just left Chloride this morning."

"Neighborly of you."

"It's the least I could do after coming near to giving you another bellybutton."

"If you want to start the fire, Raider, I'll go ahead and fetch that coffee water I was fixing to get when you pulled in."

Bennett went into a corner and acted like he was trying to make himself invisible while the other two men went about the camp chores.

CHAPTER THIRTY-FIVE

Raider's eyes narrowed. It was morning, eight or nine judging by the sun, and the night chill had long since given way to the day's growing heat.

Raider stood at one of the narrow gun ports and looked down the remnants of the Mormon Road to the south. A benchlike step had been built along the inside of the fort wall to give defenders a better field of view outside, and this helped him now to spot the moving figures coming in off the desert.

Dark specks against a paler background at first, the shapes slowly separated themselves into three. Slowly they drew close enough that he could see. One horseman and two led animals. One of the led horses was burdened with a pack. The other, obviously a spare mount, was unencumbered.

And the rider... Elbert Smith, Jr., who used to be called Billy?

The man was still too far away to identify.

Raider turned and glanced at his companions inside the tumbledown old fort.

Bennett, still in handcuffs, although now his wrists were pinioned in front of his belly so he could feed himself while they sat and waited, was sitting on Loon Michaels' pack frame. Bennett wore a glum, hangdog expression. He acted like a man who knew that his day to die had dawned.

The big prospector was adding fuel to the fire he had maintained ever since they woke this morning, brewing yet another pot of the thick, grounds-gritty coffee that he seemed to be addicted to. He had cheerfully shared his first two pots of the morning with Raider and Bennett. This third boiling—and of the same grounds, at that—he would have to drink by himself as far as Raider was concerned.

"Company comin'," Raider observed quietly.

Bennett looked like he wanted to cry.

Michaels looked up with interest. "That fella you told me about?"

"Maybe. Too far away yet to be sure." Raider picked up the Winchester he had bought in Chloride and visually inspected it to make sure it was fully loaded and properly functioning. He already knew that it was, of course, but the verification was a habit and not a bad one.

"You want some help?" Michaels offered.

Raider winked at him. "Only if I need it."

Loon looked disappointed again. First no hanging. Now no gunfight. What a waste of opportunities.

"Anyhow it might not be him. Won't know f'r sure till I get a good look at him."

"You figure you'll know 'im if you see 'im?"

Raider shrugged. But he had to believe that he would. Surely no one would go to all this trouble and expense without almighty fine reason. The man who now called himself Smith must surely be someone whose path Raider had crossed before.

Pale fella, Bennett had said. A recently released jailbird, then? Possible. Possible too that Raider had been the one to put him there. Otherwise why enough hatred for him to want Raider's head as a plaything.

"We'll let him ride around to the front and dismount. Get nice and close so I can see him," Raider said.

"Be glad to take a hand in it with you," Michaels said.

"I appreciate it, Loon. Let's see what happens."

Michaels nodded, cheered by that slim possibility that he might get into the action, and pulled the pot of simmering coffee away from the center of the bed of coals. Raider guessed he didn't want it to boil over and be lost while Smith/Billy was being braced.

Bennett stared down toward his toes and refused to look at his captor. He seemed resigned to his fate now, didn't even try to tell Raider any more lies about his innocence in the scheme.

The rider and horses nearer the outside wall, heading toward the same gap that Raider had used to gain entrance to the yard inside the remains of the old fort.

Raider grimaced.

This was Smith, all right.

"Bill Setton," he mumbled.

"What?"

"Smith. That's him. His real name is Bill Setton. William Randolph Setton if I remember right. Confidence artist. He had a plan going that was supposed to earn him a fortune and make him some kinda silly emperor down in Mexico a few years back. Me and a fella I used to partner burst his bubble for him and sent him off to Yuma Prison. Sure as hell thought we'd recovered all the money he stole, but I bet we didn't. He's bankrolled right well again now." Raider shook his head.

"Setton didn't used to be a killer. Confidence men generally ain't. I expect prison life changed him some."

Bill Setton and his horses passed out of sight from the gun port, and Raider moved over to the doorway where he could stand in the shadows and wait for a good chance to take Setton. Again.

"You gonna shoot him?" Michaels asked.

"Only if I got to, Loon. I'd ruther not." Raider slouched against the doorjamb and patiently waited for Setton to show himself.

There were horses out there and smoke rising to show that the place was being occupied at the moment, but Raider doubted that would put Setton off. He probably knew that the old fort was a commonly used shelter.

Raider wiped his palm across his jeans and earred back the hammer of the Winchester.

The rattle of hoofs on stony debris announced the arrival of these new guests at the impromptu inn.

Just a few more yards now. A dozen steps or so. That was all Raider needed for a clean line of fire. Once he was into the yard, Setton wouldn't have anyplace to hide. He would have to give himself up or go down.

Easy pickings, Raider thought with pleasure. Unlike Loon Michaels, he would rather have this end smooth and simple and no powder burned.

He raised the rifle toward his shoulder as Setton and the horses reached the edge of the yard.

"Save me, Smith, he's gonna kill us all!"

The shriek tore out of Buddy Bennett's throat, and the terrified fat man launched himself across the floor toward Raider's back.

Out in the yard Setton yanked on his reins and tried to wheel hard away from the warning.

"Shit!" Raider snarled.

He ducked as a still screaming and incoherent Buddy Bennett tried to reach him.

Raider jumped forward into the sunlight, Winchester

at the ready now. He had no time to deal with Bennett.

Setton had spun his saddle horse into the trailing animals, snarling the lead rope that was tied to his saddle horn and frightening all three animals into a panic.

"Halt! You're under arrest." That was the right thing to say, but it sounded stupid even as he hollered it. Halt. You bet. Bill Setton was really gonna do that now.

Setton was frantically trying to throw the lead rope off his horn so he could free the horse he was riding and trying at the same time to take aim at Raider with a small pistol.

The pistol barked, the crack of the gunshot sharp but not particularly loud.

Raider took aim at the man on the back of the plunging, frightened horse.

The packhorse reared and squealed just as Raider's finger tightened.

The Winchester roared and rocked back against Raider's shoulder, but it was the packhorse that went down with a bullet in its head instead of Bill Setton.

Raider heard a thump and a crash behind him, but he had no time to think about it now. He levered another cartridge into the Winchester and snapped off a hurried shot that sprayed adobe clay into the air as Setton finally got loose of the other animals, the one dead one and the other panicked one, and spurred his mount out through the gap toward the desert.

"Aw, shit!"

Raider spun and ran back inside the fort.

He had to jump over a limp body lying inert in the doorway. Bennett, he saw in passing. Loon Michaels was standing nearby with a grin on his face. Loon had gotten to help out after all.

Raider ran to the nearest gun port and jumped onto the firing step. He pushed the muzzle of the Winchester outside, his eyes flicking back and forth already as he searched for his target.

There.

Raider fired. Too soon. The slug hit the ground, raising a splash of dirt, and whined off into the distance.

Setton saw or heard and realized the danger. A run toward the south would expose his back to Raider's rifle fire.

And most bullets can handily outrun even the swiftest horse.

Setton reined hard to the left to put the adobe walls of the fort between himself and Raider's fire.

Raider cussed and tried to line his sights onto Setton, but it was no use. The gun port was too narrow to permit the extreme angle of fire this close to the walls.

"*Damn* it!" Raider snarled.

He turned back to the room and grabbed for his saddle. He should've known better, damn it. He shouldn't be this late in the damn day with his horse unsaddled.

Hindsight was wonderful. But ineffective.

"Get him, Raider."

"Thanks, Loon." Raider paused and looked at what was lying in the doorway. "Lordy, but you do hit hard, don't you?"

Michaels just grinned at him.

Buddy Bennett had been right about this being his day to die. The side of his skull was split open like a rotten melon. Raider had no idea what Michaels had hit him with when he tried to jump Raider, but it had sure as hell done the job.

No time to worry about a dead man now. Raider scooped up a bag of supplies and raced outside with it and his saddle.

Setton was riding hell-for-leather away from there, and Raider didn't want to be far behind.

Raider dashed to the makeshift corral and grabbed the best of the horses he and Bennett had brought from Chloride. He threw his saddle on the first one he touched and hurriedly began snapping cinch straps.

Michaels was only a few steps behind him, and the big man was carrying every canteen the three men had had among them. Including his own.

"Bring these back when you're done with them, Raider. I'll wait here for you."

Raider hesitated for a moment, looking into the big prospector's eyes. Then he nodded grimly and accepted the help Loon was giving him.

It was a damned decent thing Loon was doing. Without his canteens he was pretty much trapped here at the fort until Raider came back. Either that or quit his prospecting trip and make a dry and possibly dangerous trip to buy more water containers.

"Thanks, Loon." Raider slung the straps of the canteens over his horn and gathered up the lead rope of his spare mount.

Setton only had the one horse now. Raider having two would be an advantage.

"You want I should go ahead an' bury Bennett?"

"I'd appreciate it, Loon."

"See y' later then, Raider. Good luck."

Raider swung into his saddle and rode out past the body of Setton's dead packhorse. The other horse Setton had been leading was calming now and trying to get inside the enclosure to join the other horses there.

Raider headed out onto the old road and turned north. He could see Bill Setton's dust far ahead of him there.

Raider clucked and put his horses into motion. Not at a run, though. He held them to a smooth lope instead. This would be a race, all right. A race to the death. But in this contest it would be endurance that would win out, not bursts of initial speed.

He loped smooth and steady toward the northern horizon.

CHAPTER THIRTY-SIX

The sun climbed higher onto Raider's right shoulder, camped a while at the back of his neck, and began sliding down over his left shoulder as the road held to its northerly course.

He wasn't much closer to Setton now than when he'd started.

That was all right.

This kind of chase could take days to complete. Raider was confident he would win it.

He stopped just past noon to switch his saddle again and let the horses crop some of the meager forage that was available to them. He ate a piece of jerky and walked idly in slow circles just to keep his circulation going, then recovered the reins and lead rope and once more set out at the steady and relentless road jog he had been holding to for hours.

Setton's dust was barely visible to the north. He had gained some distance while Raider and his horses rested.

That distance didn't matter. Setton hadn't stopped, and his one horse had gotten no rest.

This evening, tomorrow . . . it didn't matter.

Raider and his two mounts loped slowly forward.

"Well, now," Raider said aloud. The horse he was riding twitched its ears.

Night had slowed but not stopped him.

But then Bill Setton had slowed too. And it wasn't because of the night.

Raider was closing the gap between them at a steady pace now, as Setton's flagging horse was unable to hold to the killing pace Setton was trying to force onto it.

There was enough light in the clear night sky for Raider to see the black shape of horse and rider far ahead.

Except not so very far now as it had been.

Raider had to admire the strength of Setton's horse. The man might be a son of a bitch, but the animal was magnificent.

Most would have dropped dead before now.

Raider wondered how much water Setton had with him. He hadn't taken time to look at the trappings on the pack animal back at the fort. Likely, though, much of his water had been carried on the packhorse. He probably didn't have more than a canteen with him, perhaps two. Almost certainly no more than that.

And the ignorant asshole hadn't stopped in hours to let his horse water and blow.

Raider drew his own horses to a stop again, switched the saddle once more, and uncapped one of the canteens Loon Michaels had thoughtfully brought out to him.

He spilled some of the refreshing, life-giving water onto his bandanna and used the dripping-wet cloth to moisten and clean the mouths and the nostrils of both his horses.

Only when that had been done did he take a spare sip for himself.

He unbuttoned his fly and took a leak while he had the chance, then buttoned up again and swung onto the saddle.

Setton and his horse were almost lost in the darkness ahead.

Almost but not quite.

Raider kneed his horse forward, the spare animal obediently following at the end of the lead rope.

It would be dawn soon. Raider could see a pale glow lining the horizon to the east.

There was a starkly black lump marring the flat, mostly featureless shape of that horizon.

Raider realized with something of a surprise that he recognized the shape.

Those were the Virgin Mountains over there. He'd approached them in the night without realizing they had ridden so far. It was a helluva distance from the Mormon Fort to the Virgins. And the road had swung more to the northeast than he'd realized.

Lordy, but that horse of Bill Setton's was a stayer.

If there was any justice at all in this world, Raider thought, that horse would survive the ride Setton was giving it.

Setton might not, damn him, but Raider hoped the horse would live through it. An animal like that deserved better than this.

He couldn't believe the thing was still on its feet and moving forward.

It was slow now, of course. Only a few hundred yards away.

Raider's horses were both still fresh. He could throw the spurs and catch up with Setton anytime he wanted.

He decided to wait a bit longer. Until the dawn, when there would be better light to fight by. Setton might or might not want to put up a resistance. The choice would be his.

Raider had to actually slow the pace of his two horses so he would not overrun Setton.

He sat back against his cantle and waited for the dawn.

Son of a bitch, they really had come a ways.

Raider could see the Blue Walls standing empty and lonesome ahead of him as the first light flooded over the Virgins and down onto the desert floor.

Setton was only a hundred yards ahead of Raider now.

His horse was staggering, its feet paddling. It lurched sideways, dropping in the loins and nearly unseating its rider, then righted itself and plodded forward one step more and one more after that.

This had gone far enough, Raider thought. Fuck Bill Setton. He wanted to save that horse.

He bumped his own mount into a swift lope and swept out to the right, leaving the road and galloping in a circle to place himself between Setton and the shelter the Blue Walls could have offered.

He didn't need a lengthy siege with Setton under cover and Raider having to wait him out.

Setton saw what Raider was doing and lashed his horse, whipping it with his rein ends and jabbing it with his spurs.

The gallant animal tried to respond. It lifted its head and pinned its ears and tried to shuffle forward quicker, but it had no more to give.

The big-hearted horse raised its muzzle to the sky, shivered, and crashed down to the earth.

"Christ," Raider said.

He glowered at the SOB who had done this to so magnificent an animal as that one had been.

Raider dragged his Winchester out of the scabbard and pulled his horse to a stop as Setton scrambled off his saddle and began running toward the protection of the Blue Walls.

"Stop, damn you."

Raider fired a warning shot in front of Setton's boots.

The man stumbled and fell to his knees a good fifty yards short of the Blue Walls.

Raider dismounted and moved toward him on foot. "Give it up, Setton."

"Never." Setton reached into his pocket and pulled out an undersized, nickle-plated revolver that he waved threateningly.

Raider damn near laughed. That pipsqueak little sonuvabitch pistol was small danger at belly-to-belly distance. And none at all from this range.

"You want that bad to die, Setton, I reckon I might have to accommodate you." He hefted the Winchester. At this distance he could put bullets into Bill Setton as accurately as a carpenter driving nails into a coffin lid. "What I think you oughta do, though, is toss that thing down and give yourself up. Hell, man, you know Yuma good enough to make yourself comfortable there. They'll be glad to have you home again."

"I'm going to kill you, damn you. I'm going to hang your head from a rafter and spit into your face every day. Yours and that stinking Weatherbee's, too. Damn you both for what you did to me."

The fella sure was worked up about this, Raider thought calmly. Never had figured out that it was him that was out of step and not the whole rest of the world.

"I'd still ruther take you in than put you down, Setton. But I reckon you've the right to choose."

"Fuck you, Raider."

Raider began walking forward.

Setton was still on his knees in the dirt. He looked wildly around, head snapping back and forth, useless little pistol jerking in all directions, eyes bugged out huge and glassy. He looked like a weasel trapped in the bottom of a tin pail.

Then, unexpectedly, he stopped and stared and began to smile.

He looked back at Raider, and his chest puffed out triumphantly.

"I told you I'd have your head, Raider, and so I shall, damn you."

Raider looked in the direction where Setton had been staring. Toward the Blue Walls.

There were people coming out into sight from the old building, men first, and one of them was carrying a Winchester rifle cradled against his chest.

The men first, then the women, then the two kids.

Bill Setton knew them, all right.

But so did Raider.

The question was, would the Indian band side with Raider? Or with the man who had promised to pay them riches beyond their wildest imaginings.

Setton lurched to his feet and wildly pointed in Raider's direction. "Kill him. Kill him now. I'll pay you double what we already agreed. Kill him now."

The headman grunted and turned to the young woman who spoke English, then looked back at Setton and smiled.

He jacked the lever of the Winchester that had been Raider's.

CHAPTER THIRTY-SEVEN

"No!" Raider barked, but he was too late. And he had taught the headman entirely too well how to handle a Winchester rifle.

The headman aimed swiftly and squeezed the trigger.

The slug crashed into Bill Setton's breastbone and threw him backward with sledgehammer force.

"You didn't hafta do that," Raider complained.

The headman was looking at him and grinning happily. The Indian patted the Winchester that had been Raider's and stroked it as gently as if it had been a favorite bedmate's tit.

He said something in his own language. Raider didn't really need a translation. The headman sounded proud. And courteous. A favor had been owed. Now a debt had been paid. The white man who wanted the band's friend killed was dead now. Thank you very much for the rifle and the meat.

"Right," Raider said.

He walked over to Setton's body, but there wasn't really much point in it.

The man was dead as dead ever gets. The headman's aim had been quick and true.

Lordy, but these ignorant, uncivilized savages—as nearly everybody would think of them, anyhow—were awful good at whatever they learned how to do, whether it be soft-footing it through the dark without a sound or killing jackrabbits with no more than a bent stick for a weapon—or learning how to shoot a thoroughly modern high-powered rifle.

They were survivors, that was for damn sure.

The rest of the band gathered around now to greet Raider with smiles and touches on his arms and shy pride.

There were two more of them than he'd seen before now. Both the strangers to him were women older than the headman. When they led him over to the Blue Walls he could see why. The two women had stayed behind when the rest of the band went chasing Raider into the desert. They'd salvaged meat from the dead horses Raider had thought rotten and useless, and now strips of horseflesh were drying on the stone walls of the old corral.

It occurred to Raider that if the Indians were that hard up for meat they might just as well have the use of everything they could get.

He excused himself with a smile and walked out to the horse that SOB Setton had killed on his way here.

The animal was down but still breathing.

Raider knelt by its head and pulled his knife out to cut its throat.

The sweat-caked horse tried to rise for him, struggled gamely, but couldn't make it.

"Aw, shit," Raider complained.

He got back onto his feet and ran over to his own horse, got a canteen, and hurried back to the magnificent bay. He tipped water into its mouth, then wet his bandanna and swabbed its nostrils, too.

A shadow moved over him and he looked up. The Indian girl was there. "Will live," she said. There wasn't any question in her tone of voice. She sounded sure.

Raider nodded.

He *wanted* this horse to survive, damn it.

The animal had earned that much.

He looked over to where the horse he'd been leading was picking at the wisps of dry grass and browse it could find on the desert.

"I'll keep this one," he told her. "Your people can have that one for meat."

She let out a yelp and ran to tell the rest of the band.

The bay struggled again, and this time with Raider's help it fought its way onto its feet.

He could stay here a day or two to let the bay rest and recuperate, Raider decided. The delay would be worthwhile, and Loon wouldn't mind.

In the meantime, maybe he could talk the headman into swapping back Raider's own trusted Winchester in exchange for the new one he'd bought in Chloride. Hell, he could give the Indians all the spare ammunition he was carrying and whatever they wanted of Setton's gear.

Yeah, he decided, that would work.

He rubbed the bay's neck and let it drink a little from the upended crown of his hat, then turned it loose so it could rest.

He walked over to join the Indians. The little boy had already run out to claim the horse Raider had given them and lead it in for slaughter.

There'd been a lot of slaughtering going on lately, but at least this kind was for a good cause.

Raider smiled when the headman came over to him and once again laid the palm of his hand against Raider's chest in a gesture of friendship.

It never hurt a man, Raider realized, to have friends, even ones found in strange places.

"Thank you," Raider told him. The girl didn't bother translating that. But then, he suspected she didn't have to. Raider placed his palm on the headman's chest and smiled.

The hard-hitting, gun-slinging Pride of the Pinkertons rides solo in this action-packed series.

J.D. HARDIN'S
RAIDER

Sharpshooting Pinkertons Doc and Raider are legends in their own time, taking care of outlaws that the local sheriffs can't handle. Doc has decided to settle down and now Raider takes on the nastiest vermin the Old West has to offer single-handedly...charming the ladies along the way.

___THE ANDERSON VALLEY SHOOT-OUT #22	0-425-11542-9/$2.95
___THE YELLOWSTONE THIEVES #24	0-425-11619-0/$2.95
___THE ARKANSAS HELLRIDER #25	0-425-11650-6/$2.95
___BORDER WAR #26	0-425-11694-8/$2.95
___THE EAST TEXAS DECEPTION #27	0-425-11749-9/$2.95
___DEADLY AVENGERS #28	0-425-11786-3/$2.95
___HIGHWAY OF DEATH #29	0-425-11839-8/$2.95
___THE PINKERTON KILLERS #30	0-425-11883-5/$2.95
___TOMBSTONE TERRITORY #31	0-425-11920-3/$2.95
___MEXICAN SHOWDOWN #32	0-425-11972-6/$2.95
___THE CALIFORNIA KID #33	0-425-12011-2/$2.95
___BORDER LAW #34	0-425-12055-4/$2.95
___HANGMAN'S LAW #35	0-425-12097-X/$2.95
___FAST DEATH #36	0-425-12138-0/$2.95
___DESERT DEATH TRAP #37	0-425-12175-5/$2.95
___WYOMING AMBUSH #38	0-425-12222-0/$2.95
___KILLER'S MOON #39 (Sept. '90)	0-425-12271-9/$2.95

Check book(s). Fill out coupon. Send to:

BERKLEY PUBLISHING GROUP
390 Murray Hill Pkwy., Dept. B
East Rutherford, NJ 07073

NAME_____

ADDRESS_____

CITY_____

STATE_____ZIP_____

PLEASE ALLOW 6 WEEKS FOR DELIVERY.
PRICES ARE SUBJECT TO CHANGE
WITHOUT NOTICE.

POSTAGE AND HANDLING:
$1.00 for one book, 25¢ for each additional. Do not exceed $3.50.

BOOK TOTAL $____

POSTAGE & HANDLING $____

APPLICABLE SALES TAX $____
(CA, NJ, NY, PA)

TOTAL AMOUNT DUE $____

PAYABLE IN US FUNDS.
(No cash orders accepted.)

208c

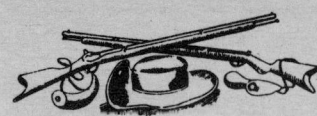

A special offer for people who enjoy reading the best Westerns published today. If you enjoyed this book, subscribe now and get...

TWO FREE WESTERNS!
A $5.90 VALUE—NO OBLIGATION

If you enjoyed this book and would like to read more of the very best Westerns being published today, you'll want to subscribe to True Value's Western Home Subscription Service. If you enjoyed the book you just read and want more of the most exciting, adventurous, action packed Westerns, subscribe now.

TWO FREE BOOKS

When you subscribe, we'll send you your first month's shipment of the newest and best 6 Westerns for you to preview. With your first shipment, two of these books will be yours as our introductory gift to you absolutely FREE, regardless of what you decide to do.

Special Subscriber Savings

As a True Value subscriber all regular monthly selections will be billed at the low subscriber price of just $2.45 each. That's at least a savings of $3.00 each month below the publishers price. There is never any shipping, handling or other hidden charges. What's more there is no minimum number of books you must buy, you may return any selection for full credit and you can cancel your subscription at any time. A TRUE VALUE!

Mail the coupon below

To start your subscription and receive 2 FREE WESTERNS, fill out the coupon below and mail it today. We'll send your first shipment which includes 2 FREE BOOKS as soon as we receive it.

Mail To: True Value Home Subscription Services, Inc.
P.O. Box 5235
120 Brighton Road
Clifton, New Jersey 07015-5235

12175

YES! I want to start receiving the very best Westerns being published today. Send me my first shipment of 6 Westerns for me to preview FREE for 10 days. If I decide to keep them, I'll pay for just 4 of the books at the low subscriber price of $2.45 each; a total of $9.80 (a $17.70 value). Then each month I'll receive the 6 newest and best Westerns to preview Free for 10 days. If I'm not satisfied I may return them within 10 days and owe nothing. Otherwise I'll be billed at the special low subscriber rate of $2.45 each; a total of $14.70 (at least a $17.70 value) and save $3.00 off the publishers price. There are never any shipping, handling or other hidden charges. I understand I am under no obligation to purchase any number of books and I can cancel my subscription at any time, no questions asked. In any case the 2 FREE books are mine to keep.

Name _____

Address _____ Apt. # _____

City _____ State _____ Zip _____

Telephone # _____

Signature _____
(if under 18 parent or guardian must sign)

Terms and prices subject to change. Orders subject to acceptance by True Value Home Subscription Services, Inc.